THE
CULT TRACKER
CHRONICLES

BOOK TWO

Melanie's Tainted Casket

R. SCOTT REATH

This book is dedicated to all of those who stood against tyranny, whether they were in the military, public figures, comedians, or employees who stood against oppressive regimes in corporate culture. These thoughts were penned with you in mind.

TABLE OF CONTENTS

-Often the most terrifying things about human beings
are what they believe-

CHAPTER I

MUSICAL DIFFERENCES

Ray and Wade rose early to get a head start on the day, as they had a fair distance to travel before noticing that their neighbors had carved a large letter "A" with a circle around it in the paint on the hood of their car.

"Again?" Ray asked incredulously.

The new loft was perfect for their headquarters: lots of space, a great price, and out of the way from prying eyes among a series of abandoned factories. They had celebrated their auspicious surroundings several times before they discovered their neighbors and how easily they could be provoked into a series of feuds over next to nothing. They were reluctant to participate at first, but the stakes kept increasing.

"Taking the high road doesn't seem to be helping our cause, does it?" Wade asked.

The two men locked eyes and walked across the parking area, and Ray pulled out a hunting knife and began jabbing the tires of all the vehicles parked in front of the illegally occupied factory across the grounds.

Wade took a screwdriver and thrust it into the corner of each windshield with just enough force to leave a chip with spider line cracks that didn't impede the driver's view but would require replacing in order to be driven legally.

"I'll leave Stan and Jake a text in case the Natives wake up restless," Ray said.

"Given that we have a Cherokee woman and two half Natives among us, that means *we are* the Natives," Wade said.

"We should go carve the word 'democracy' across their door," Ray smiled.

"Oh, I think they'll be plenty pissed already," Wade said.

The two men took the highway southwest, listening to 70s rock and letting the rushing breeze take their minds off of the sordid business at hand. After about an hour, Ray shut the stereo off and grimaced a little.

"I know this isn't just another case for you," he said.

Wade stayed silent.

"I'm not a big fan of nosy questions, so if I get annoying, just tell me," he said.

Wade stared straight ahead beneath his Western-styled fedora, which he always felt added a bit of maturity to his look, and it was a nod to old detective movies as well. The police might think him out of date, but they rarely became aggressive at the sight of a fedora.

"You waived the fee in case we don't find her, so that's new. You agree to go meet them at their home at our expense, on a long shot, and you're dressed businesslike. I'm just saying that I've never seen this before. You want to tell me what time it is, or should I just go and buy myself a new watch and pretend I've always gone by the sun's position?" Ray asked.

"I'm sure she's dead," Wade said slowly.

"On account of...?"

"These folks aren't rich, but they have more than the average. They've talked to every force and agency in the book and have probably hired ten private investigators, and they've never caught a whiff. Some of those guys may be scammers, but a lot of them won't drop a case until they find out about every granny's aborted stepchild," Wade grunted.

"So we're just chasing our tails, then, for the fun of it?"

"My curiosity is piqued," Wade said, looking less than comfortable with the subject.

"Okay, Wade, so then we go, but something feels way off about this," Ray said.

Back at The Pitt, the over-aged punk rockers had gathered outside equipped with tire irons, steel-toed boots, a few bicycle chains, and lead pipes.

Stan and Jake went outside to meet their oppressors with aluminum baseball bats, but the cook, Angel, quickly followed, brandishing a long kitchen knife and a look on her face that suggested she was more than ready to use it. The punks numbered about fifteen, and they were boiling mad.

"Ay, you fucks want to tell us what happened to our cars last night?" A grizzled punk with an ankh in his cheek shouted.

Stan grinned at them, while Jake glared.

"I dunno, there seems to be a problem with vandals in the neighborhood; we've had our doors wrecked, painted on, and our windows broken. Any idea who might be out to deface our property?" Jake asked.

"Probably someone heard your shitty hippie music playin' and couldn't take it anymore," a steely-eyed agitator with black eyebrows proudly flaunting his burnt orange Mohawk shouted.

"First of all, it's not shitty music because they actually know how to play their instruments, and it passed the test of time. You idiots want music by guys who can't even play their instruments! Same matching haircuts are your sole criteria; that's some serious boy band bullshit right there! You get to imitate the people stupid enough to pierce their own faces, so fucking cool!" Jake said, raising his voice.

"How'd you like to get boot fucked?" The punk roared back with eyes bulging madly, as he seethed unable to slow his mounting rage.

"Naw, I leave that for the chicks; you know, the ones that like lots of jewelry, just like you guys," Jake said, escalating his tone again.

Although Jake was tallest at six foot six, it was Stan who cast the most intimidating shadow, and people sometimes said he had "shark eyes" as he rarely ever blinked. As the first punk rushed Jake, Stan cut him off in his tracks with a switch kick, throwing up his left leg first but lurching forward with his right leg as it snapped crisply under the jaw of the punk with the Mohawk as his head tilted upward at an odd angle and he fell to the dirt wordlessly, without getting up. His friends helped up the dazed husk of a man.

"This isn't over!" A grizzled punk shouted waving his gloved fist with spiked knuckles.

"Aw, gotta regroup first?" Stan asked with a sneer.

"Yeah, come back! And I'll cut ya's all up and feed you to the boys for dinner!" Angel screeched, waving her knife maniacally.

As they returned to The Pitt, the walk was silent. Once inside, the mood lifted a little.

"You are a good girlfriend, one who stands up in support of her man, feisty, but only when it's called for. I like that. I think we might stay together until we get old; I really do, but, as of now I'm going to be checking all of the meat you cook for face jewelry," Jake said dryly.

"You're good too, and I might even stay with you that long, but if you don't watch your mouth, you'll be eating roast punk boot leather," Angel said, waving her wooden spoon at him.

Later, Ray pulled up to a driveway in Cedar Hill Valley, and Wade emerged grim faced. He rang the bell, squinting, and a man of about sixty opened the door with dark hair and horn-rimmed glasses.

"Please come in," he said.

It was a split-level home with antique furniture and elegant decor. There was a grand piano in the living room, antique oil paintings, and treated wooden art that read messages like "Hope, Kindness, and Humility."

"We appreciate you coming," a woman with premature gray hair and kindly smile lines etched into her face, said. Any warmth in her eyes instantly gave way to the frosted reality of a grieving parent.

"Well, I have no wish to torment anyone with questions they've answered a thousand times, Mrs. St. James. I was wondering if I could see her room, and anything you think of that might be helpful would be appreciated," Wade said.

"Deniege! Can you show the men Mel's room, please?" Mr. St. James called out.

"Our other daughter will show you around, as we really don't like to go in there too often," the lady said.

"Of course," Wade said.

From the top of the stairs came a lovely looking woman with a long white blouse and black slacks sauntering, who had Ray's head nod up and down involuntarily in reaction to her languid, curvilinear figure. In spite of her height, she was exceedingly graceful; her feet barely touched the stairs as she descended. Wade also had an unexpected reaction, as he had to squint his eyes to keep them from bulging in recognition. This fooled no one, however, as all the color ran from his face, leaving what resembled a ghastly pale substitute version of himself trying desperately to look unfazed. She could have passed for Melanie save for her height and captivating presence. She was an absolute stunner with far more kindness and understanding in her eyes, and suddenly Wade's mind was racing for an excuse to leave in great haste.

"Are you alright?" The girl's mother asked, bringing him a glass of water.

"I'm very sorry; I saw pictures in the paper, and I wasn't expecting... I'm sorry," Wade said, forcing up his voice as his throat ran dry.

"Oh, it's quite fine; I do resemble my elder sister a tad, perhaps I should have said something to prepare you. It is I, who should apologize," she said.

Wade turned and shot Ray a glance as if to ask if he were taking note of all that was happening, and he got a miniature half-nod in response.

He remembered thinking that Melanie was the most beautiful woman he'd ever seen, how she'd revealed her chest to him when he was twelve years old, and how that image kept him up at night through all of his teenage years, despite her making it clear she held no regard for him at all.

Now, of all times, he discovered her younger sister was even more intoxicating, closer to his age, and all he wanted to do was run from this situation. He wanted to run from his pretense of a search, and her parents, from Ray's friendly suspicion, and run from a woman who could melt his sternest resolve with a mere glance. He should be back at The Pitt fighting the punks, and he never should have come here.

"Can we see your room too? Just for a comparison," Ray inquired as Wade gave him a mild glare.

"Sure, if you think it'll help," Deniege said.

"So, why do you think your sister joined a cult?" Ray asked.

"I think she was lashing out at me, my parents, the school, and society in general," she said.

"Why?" Ray asked.

"Jeez Ray, because her sister plays the piano like a virtuoso, and breezed through school without ever picking up a book. She has academic awards, has manners, and is a sure bet to be universally popular. Her parents tried their best to share their pride equally, but when one child is the star player at everything she does, it's difficult not to beam a little more pride in one direction over the other. Kids are like magnifying glasses; they drink in and amplify everything in their heads, every appreciation, and every slight." Wade said.

"Very astute; Mel was always eager for some alternate form of approval and didn't care where she got it; the more offensive, the better," Deniege said.

"Deniege? Interesting name," Ray commented.

"It means: From Snow," Wade groaned hoping to dispense with any further trivial questions.

"You seem pretty observant; do you really think you can find my sister?" Deniege asked.

"I think we are in a tough situation and want to help bring closure for the family. We always hope for the best result, but I don't like the length of time it's been. No requests for help or money, no letters, but that proves nothing. I want to bring the truth to your family, whatever it may be, so the future can be free from clouds and doubts."

"No rose-colored glasses of yours, hanging off of your nose then, are there?" Deneige asked flatly.

"I'm sorry, he is just a really blunt guy sometimes; he didn't mean anything bad," Ray said.

"Oh, it's a breath of fresh air. Do you know how much false hope people have given us over the years? I prefer honesty," she said.

"Can you tell us anything more that might help?" Ray asked.

"Well, she went dark; stealing, lighting fires, fistfights with other girls, torturing animals, drugs, the whole bit. It was like she wanted to test the limits of how bad she could become and get away with it. She was never like that toward me, though, so I held out hope, but once she started hanging out with that cult, the things they were into were even too dark for her. I know she wouldn't have been cool with it."

"Sorry, but what makes you so sure?" Ray asked.

"She told me once that everything comes full circle and that one day she was going to find the breakthrough point of evil, pass through it, find a rebirth kind of moment, and become good again," Deneige said.

Finding nothing of use in Mel's room, no diary, no weapon, no hidden meeting place addresses, they rejoined her parents in the living room. The father looked hard at Wade.

"No disrespect, but what makes you think you can find our daughter when so many others failed?"

"I don't. I think we can find out what's happened, what's become of her, where she went, and why there's been no word," Wade said.

"Why, though?"

"Because people lead messy lives, and where there's a mess, there's often something people didn't cleanup afterwards, and that's where we focus," Wade said.

The lady stood up and walked close to Wade, staring him in the eyes.

"Our daughter, did you know her?"

"I know she was caught up in something she wanted no part of, no matter how it might have started out, and I don't really know any of the people we look for, but I often imagine I know them all," he said.

"Really?" She asked unassumingly.

"We've never even been out this way before, we're Easterners," Ray smiled, before turning to Wade.

"I just got a text from Suze; it looks like some more touch-ups and remodeling of the office," he added.

"We should go," Wade said.

"We want to thank you for looking into this. Won't you take a few dollars just for expenses and gas?" Mrs. St. James asked.

"After we're certain we aren't chasing our own shadows and wrong turns," Wade smiled.

Once in the Jeep, Wade prepared for an onslaught of questions from Ray, but he asked none. They drove in silence for a few miles before Ray got a text.

"It looks like Stan KO'd one of our punk friends," he mumbled.

"Great, anything more?" Wade asked.

"No, sorry that lady got so damn nosy with you, I guess she's the type that if she'd had the Zapruder film on JFK, she would have blabbed about it to everyone she knew until she ended up lying next to him," Ray said.

"What set her off?"

"Usually you've got a solid poker face, but when you saw that girl, you turned whiter than a stripper's coke spoon, and everyone noticed," Ray said.

"Great!"

"She read it all wrong, of course, you weren't frozen, you were angry, and more than a little."

"What?" Wade asked.

"I've never seen you blanch before. You have a large adrenaline tank, and you never run, so it was fight, not flight. All that blood is leaving the normal areas, rushing to the heart and muscles, and accelerating the clotting agents in your body in case of any heavy bleeding. That can leave the face pasty white. No, you were struck by a vision or a memory. You were steamed! Physiologically fighting mad, and the only question is, why?"

"I took her for someone else, and I thought I'd been played," Wade confessed.

"Well, she's a definite looker. Maybe you knew her in another life," Ray cheerfully mocked.

"Maybe we should find a spot to get some lunch," Wade said.

"Nope, it's Suze texting; she says those punks started a fire around The Pitt, more trouble," Ray said, jerking the steering wheel violently.

"Give me your phone. I'll tell them to hold off until we get there," Wade said.

Back at The Pitt, Stan and Jake were preparing makeshift weapons along with their aluminum bats as the punks emptied large, red, plastic Jerrycans of gasoline at the front door, to the catwalk, and on the metal stairs of the fire exit. As time ticked by, they added wooden crates and debris on top of the stairs to ensure the fire would continue burning and block any exit attempts. The remaining punks were shouting and waving golf clubs, hatchets and even an antique double-headed war hammer as their leader stood outside, issuing threats with a Molotov cocktail and lighter. Inside, Jake's feisty new girlfriend and resident chef, Angel, was fuming.

"The line of work you guys are in, and no one has a gun! Are you all crazy?" she asked accusingly.

"Guns mean serious charges if you're caught with them in the wrong situation," Jake said.

"Better than ending up dead, in the wrong situation!" she shouted.

"That's it! I'm calling the cops," Suzette blurted out.

"Not a good idea," Jake muttered.

"Why the hell not?" She roared.

"Because there's twenty of 'em and they live across the lot, they won't all get arrested, and they'll be back with more than hatchets after that. We have to be smart. I'll go talk to them," Jake said.

"Oh, brilliant," Suzette said.

Stan collected some kitchen grease from Angel and poured it into a glass bottle with some lighter fluid. He nodded when it was full, before noticing Jake's disapproving glance.

"In case negotiations fail," he grinned.

Stan's lighthearted comments often ventured somewhere between gallows humor and unwavering ardor, which often rubbed people the wrong way. While his outrageous combat skills were needed, his unflappable attitude sometimes made people feel alone in emergencies, as Stan left others questioning his sanity. The more collective fears escalated, the lighter Stan's attitude became, like he was tuned to an opposite wavelength as his calm seemed detached from impending risks and that often made them feel more alone in their fears.

As Jake walked out, a Molotov cocktail shot past him and burst into flame against the metal door behind him. The lit bottle made a soft hush sailing through the air and a "Whumph!" as it ignited and exploded into a crash of tinkling, shattered glass that flew in all directions.

The overaged punk rockers recoiled as the flames rose high but quickly fell down along the door's metal frame. Stan beckoned them closer with an inviting wave of his hand, not wanting to launch his bottle of grease out of range. Jake roared at the invading group all at once.

"What's the matter? Too scared to even talk? Are ya gonna run and hide now?"

His bass voice boomed across the lot in front of their loft and echoed around the derelict factory grounds the punks had claimed. Several bald or closely shaved heads sneering shuffled closer, prepared for battle. Their uniforms were scrubbed out jeans with either construction boots or steel-toed shoes, dark t-shirts with band names on them, frayed denim vests, or studded leather jackets. They weren't sporting much facial jewelry but many hostile, bitter faces, and there were no girls to be seen among them.

A man of about forty-five years of age stepped forward, clearly filling in for the younger aggressor, whom Stan knocked out. He had long sideburns and was quieter, but just as aggressive, wearing brass knuckles on both hands. Beside him was a younger, shorter sidekick with curly hair, jagged teeth, and feeding off the bravado of the elder instigator.

"You think it's us that's scared? There's only two of you, and it's payback time, bitch."

"Payback til you eat dirt!" the sidekick echoed, grinning dementedly.

"Payback for what exactly? You guys writing anarchy symbols on our property three times a week?" Jake asked sardonically.

"With all that shitty hippie music you guys listen to, whadja expect?"

"We don't tell you guys what to listen to, or anyone else. What makes you think you're in charge of our tastes?"

"We don't listen to that shit you play! It's dinosaur, hippie-stoner bullshit, and it all sucks! We never want to hear it! You idiotic wankers!" The overaged punk insisted.

"Well, hold on a second there. You never gave us a list of songs we're allowed to play and the ones we're not. You know, in a free country and all," Jake said.

"We're stomping you guys, and all your shitty music out of the neighborhood, in case you haven't guessed yet."

"Our shitty music? You guys like no-talent losers who can't even play their instruments! It sounds like cats in a blender," Jake snorted.

"Better 'n your pretentious composer wannabees," the punk shot back.

"Primal screams aren't music, asshole."

"Neither's your hippy-dippy bullshit."

"So you're gonna enforce martial law over everyone's music while pretending you stand for anarchy?"

"Aw bollocks, get fucked! Tosser!" A bald, pierced punk sneered.

"Well there's twenty of you and no one's thrown a punch yet. Too scared, need more back up?" Jake asked.

The Jeep roared closer, with a cloud of dust building up behind it. Wade was out first, then Ray jumped out from behind the wheel.

"Who are you guys?"

"That's our backup," Jake smirked.

"You'll need a lot more than that," the punk laughed derisively.

"Doubtful," Wade said, walking up to face the punk.

"Hey, hey, look, there's no need for trouble here," Ray said.

"You're already in trouble, and you won't be getting out of it with your faces intact! Let's go!"

The punk shouted and pulled out a knife with a curved hawkbill blade, arcing his right hand in a circular motion and beckoning them toward him with his left.

"Wait! I have a better idea!" Ray shouted.

The surrounding punks had merged closer behind their new leader and were all but frothing at the mouth for a one-sided mass shit-kicking.

"Look, none of you guys want trouble with the cops, and neither do we, so the fairest thing to do is to have a one-on-one battle, and the loser can say he fell in a ditch, and no one has to get in any trouble, OK?" Ray suggested.

"Your guy is bigger than everybody here, and that other guy is some kinda martial arts expert, so no fuckin' way!" the punk scoffed.

"Look, I'm five-six, practically the smallest dude around here. If you guys are so worried about size, I'll fight your sidekick there. It'll all be fair 'n' square. If I win, you guys go find somewhere else to hang out, as you can't possibly be here legally anyway, and if he wins, we split for good. Then, you get to put up all the anarchy signs and whatever else you want," Ray said.

The knife-wielding punk looked at Ray's running shoes and his friend's steel-toed shoes before answering.

"You down, Sedge?" he asked.

"I'll kill him!" the lithe sidekick with a buzzcut said, grinning with bulging dark eyes.

There was an abandoned baseball backstop behind one of the factories that had been closed off with some wall-sized boards that made for a perfect fighting arena.

"First man out is the winner!" the dark-eyed punk shouted, raising his spiked glove.

"Keep it close at first, Ray, we don't want them to think it's not fair," Jake said.

The punks cut a hole at the top of the backstop cage and dropped their guy in, who fell upon landing but rolled into an upright position and immediately leaped up on his toes into a fighting stance. This caused a momentary trace of doubt to run across the collective expressions of Jake, Wade, and Stan.

"I think their guy has had some training," Stan said.

No one answered him.

They lowered Ray, but miscommunicated and dropped him before he was ready to land.

He fell and got up, favoring his right leg. His eager adversary wasted no time in running up to him and punching him in the stomach. As Ray bent forward from the blow, the adrenalized punk wound up and launched a soccer kick to his face that sent Ray toppling backward to the ground. He struggled to get up while the charged up punk grabbed a fistful of his hair and kneed him in the face where he'd already been kicked. Again, Ray fell backward and let out an exasperated grunt. His left cheekbone was exposed by a gash, and it was swelling fast.

"You know, if he loses, we'll have to fight all the rest of these guys, right? It's going to be prison rules: Adam's apples, eye sockets, and groin strikes... and hospital food if we don't get out of it. Maybe even a burial or three under one of these factories, so best get your A-games ready," Stan said.

As Ray desperately tried scrambling to his feet, his zealous foe timed perfect kicks to keep him from balancing. One after another, they sent him sprawling to the ground. The punk was almost toying with him as the welts on Ray's face began to multiply, spawning new ones atop the prior ones.

Ray's fighting styles were mostly boxing and "sticky hands," so he rarely used his feet. He usually just bull-rushed to avoid leg injuries, but his legs were now being routinely kicked out from under him. Ray was getting up more slowly, as the undefended kicks from steel-toed shoes were coming in furiously with no sign of letting up. Ray was getting worked over, and the surrounding punks were starving for an escalation in sadism. With soaring confidence they glared malevolently and hurled threats at his three discouraged friends. They taunted them after each blow, like hyenas laughing and squealing in delight at their cornered, dejected prey. The sinking concerns for their friend dropped to survival fears as the mob mentality grew until the stench of blood-lust filled the air. The mood rapidly devolved to the point of frenzy, as the aroused punks zealously chided and shouted lustily each time Ray kissed the dirt.

"Yeah! Bootfuck him!" and "Again!" they continued shouting, while swinging their fists and weapons in the air.

Wade began to feel as if he were a young baboon before a group of hungry lions, as they locked eyes on him and his friends; some grinning, others looking fueled for vengeance. He prepared himself psychologically, not to win a life-and-death battle, but to take down as many hostiles as possible before they got to him.

"Now, Sour Ray!" Jake shouted.

This was Ray's rarely mentioned nickname due to his mauling, brawling style that affronted the skill sets of most elite boxers named Ray. The punk in control glanced upward to decipher whether it was a coded command, and in that tenth-of-a-second delay, Ray dove and tackled him. His slippery opponent, however, had great reflexes and agility. Rather than take his adversary to the ground, Ray had to settle for pulling at one leg, prying off a shoe as his hardened rival hopped away from the tackle.

The punk had a favorite leg to kick with, and now it was shoeless, so he switched styles. He began using Tae Kwon Do snap punches and Karate-style twist punches, mostly to create the illusion of the fight still being any sort of honorable contest. Ray wrapped the shoe around his right fist and easily pulled away from the incoming attack. He was visibly relieved to finally be back on his feet and had enough of imitating a punching bag. For the first time in the fight, he lost his temper.

"Well, come on!" he muttered.

Jake worried about whether Ray had enough energy left to mount a comeback, as a big flurry might drain him completely and leave him unable to fight back. Ray raised his head high, like he was about to jump with a knee, but dropped his center of gravity at the last second and fired a merciless bomb of an uppercut. It wobbled and staggered his opponent, and then Ray tripped his new enemy, who was unable to steady his balance. Before the punk fell to the ground, Ray was already on him, and they hit the ground together in a cloud of dirt and dust. Ray's feet were his drawback, but everyone had some weakness. He pinned the brash punk beneath him and began to rain down punches with both hands, as his challenger lacked a suitable ground game and seemed clueless to escape a submission. Ray wasn't looking to submit him, however, and he continued to furiously punch away with both hands, and the shoe-wrapped fist was leaving marks almost every time it landed. Ray was ensuring that the punk came out looking worse than he did and wasn't about to let up for anyone.

The crowd was silenced in shock for a few moments but gradually started shouting, "Enough! Okay, he's done! Leave him alone, ya fuckin' ghoul!"

Wade shouted, "Submit him, Ray! It's enough!"

"He's going to get us all killed if he doesn't come up for air," Jake said.

Ray heard and put the punk in a chokehold so tight that his head began to redden and swell up before those fearsome dark eyes from moments ago glazed over and rolled upward, as he lost consciousness. Ray's anger hadn't yet dissipated. He continued squeezing with his eyes closed and his forearms still locked tightly around the neck of a limp body.

"Ray! He's done! Get out of there!" Jake shouted, his voice cracking into a high-pitched, piercing sound.

Ray was so exhausted he could barely climb the frost fence of the backstop, even at a slowed rate, as the crowd turned its eyes to Ray's three supporters with no one to adjudicate for them.

Wade and Jake helped Ray out of the improvised cage while Stan watched the crowd for the first aggressor. All eyes were on Jake, the biggest of the four, but some averted Stan as he had an almost unearthly aura about him that made him far more intimidating. He stood firm, albeit wild-eyed, fists outstretched like some twisted sentinel from another realm. The sound of sirens in the distance provided no solace during a prolonged standoff of stare-downs as Jake and Wade stood back-to-back to prepare for side scramble attacks until the crowd of frustrated punks finally dispersed.

The humiliated punk with the orange Mohawk that Stan had knocked out approached in an attempt to reclaim his prior bravado, sneered, "We know where you live!"

CHAPTER 2

PARTIAL DISCL⊕SURE

The new version of The Pitt, was comfortable and laid-back and had a businesslike front entrance for clients and a spacious recreation room upstairs. It offset the foreboding atmosphere of being set among a series of abandoned factories and denizens from the outskirts of society. The interior had a far more inviting ambience, but on this day, debates over the acquisition of firearms permeated every corner of the room.

"If they're armed and we're not, then we all die," Angel said flatly.

"When cops come to a scene, the people with the guns get arrested first, no chance to parlay out of it," Suzette countered.

"There's licenses, registering, and the potential for shootouts, a countdown to someone dying, and a life on the run," Jake added.

"Ya can't show up to a gunfight with hockey sticks and baseball bats," Angel said with arms folded.

"We're scrappy guys, and scrappy guys have fuses. We already have to walk a fine line. We mess with cults, and most of the time they have so many other options available to them that they don't even need guns. Then they can point out our guns, say we were the heavies, and use their financial clout to get us all put away," Ray said.

"The milder religious cults might, but what about the *other* kind?" Angel implored.

"We've done pretty well so far," Stan said.

"She's right, you were all five minutes away from getting gang-massacred or thrown in jail, and that was just from our freakin' neighbors!" Suzette shouted.

"If we'd been armed, we wouldn't have slipped away from the cops," Wade said.

"So you guys let Ray get shit-kicked 'til he's unrecognizable before his 'Hail Mary' win decides the day, and you think that's sustainable over the long haul?" Suzette said.

"I won, didn't I?" Ray snapped.

"Yes, Ray, congratulations! You probably don't even have brain damage," Suzette said, glaring at her boyfriend.

"We should take a vote then, on the condition that no one ever brings this up again," Jake said.

"We'll give Wade two votes to prevent a draw," Stan said, to a group of nodding heads.

Stan, Angel, and Ray opted for firearms, while Jake and Suzette stood against them.

"Wade?" Jake asked.

The imagination is a potent tool, and it wasn't more than a second or two that Wade drifted deeply into his. At an accelerated pace, his mind's eye replayed that life-altering day. He extended Melanie's life for an hour, thinking he'd saved her. He was twelve, and her tormentors weren't about to surrender before a child holding a rifle. The scene had played over in his mind so many times that he could envision it playing on fast-forward without missing a detail.

Ozul wasn't a true Satanist, but a sociopath who could master the role to enable his perverse sadism and let it run amok. Melanie partially worked free of her restraints and shot the two riflemen with the .357 Wade smuggled to her. Merciless Ozul was lusting to award her death, and only a fraction of a second stood between who would fall dead first. Wade knew how to shoot, but never wanted to kill anyone. The rapidly evaporating window of time was immediate, impartial, and cold. Life would end or continue depending on the next millisecond, so he fired and would never forget the suddenness of how Ozul's frightening intensity and imposing presence ceased forever with one loud crack from a rifle. The image of his left eyebrow imploding into his cavernous forehead beneath a spray of pink mist was followed by a huge globule of blood running down his face. His body slumped to the ground, as stationary as a stone, before the echo of the shot subsided. Wade's terror was replaced with the long-lasting dread of consequences, police, and being discovered as a runaway, which kept him sleeping lightly permanently. Those troubling thoughts paled, however, against the guilt of having been oblivious to her wounds and unwittingly leaving her to die, as she claimed she simply wanted to rest. She'd saved him, but he couldn't save her, and now he had to find a way to tell her anguished family.

"Wade! Which way do you vote?" Suze asked.

"I vote for intelligence; I am pro-gun in nature and philosophy, even if just to protect society from bad governments. For our purposes, I prefer to do what the cults do: they use everything else ecxept guns and then only as a last resort. So if anyone wants to get one and lock it up in a safe, no problem. As a policy, though, we are not going to use them—not for missions, not for props, and not to intimidate opposition. That would be begging for trouble. You get a key safe, and Jakey holds the keys. One, he voted against it, and two, he doesn't drink. If he lets you get it out, we'll know it's for good reason. I think reasons such as target practice, a life-and-death emergency, or home defense only. Sound fair enough?" Wade asked.

What shaped up to be a day of raging arguments fell into a series of naps, TV, and long hours of strategizing about what to tell Melanie's parents. He quietly asked for any proof of Melanie's death via research, knowing how thin the results would be for another "Jane Doe" lost among a sea of unknown souls whose lives were spent early and never recognized.

"I'm going back to the St. James residence; I think their daughter is dead, and I don't want to drag this on any longer," Wade announced.

The room fell quiet as looks of consternation bounced from face to face.

"Aren't we a little short on evidence?" Stan asked.

"Usually we bring proof over opinion, right?" Jake asked.

"I hit the computer pretty hard last night. I'm satisfied she's gone," Wade said.

"OK, but usually we go to the last known location, dig around asking questions, and the whole bit," Ray said.

"I'll bring Suze to break it to the women; sometimes these things are easier to hear from one of their own," Wade said dismissively.

"All this compassion suddenly—you're ruining my image of you being a cold-blooded reptile; now what am I supposed to think?" Suze joked, but no one laughed.

In the Jeep, Suze proved to be in good humor and might have even felt a little more valued and appreciated than usual, given she was the one who opposed the stripper girlfriends, the guns, the fisticuffs, and numerous other actions within the group. They laughed a little at first, but as the road wound forward, Suze grew more serious.

"Do you remember that wealthy girl, Monica, the one with a D.A. for a father that I really hit it off with?"

"Of course."

"Well, I've tried to reach her a thousand times, and at first she just said she was busy with university, and now she won't even answer my texts. Do you think anything is wrong? Like, maybe we should go check on her or something?" Suze asked.

"No," Wade said.

"Why not?"

"Well, I was hoping your boyfriend Ray would have this conversation with you, but I guess it falls on me."

"Whaaaat?" Suze said, slowly dragging out the word.

"Sometimes people's priorities change in university, and wealthy people like to be charming and assure us that we are liked because that's just the mannerly thing to do. It's possible they had a good belly laugh at all of us after we left, but they were displaying a show of gratitude more than any genuine affection toward us," Wade said.

"You mean all that warmth was just a... performance?"

"Possibly. I'm sorry."

"And you guys all knew this and didn't even tell me?"

"We weren't certain and didn't want to go around espousing theories that might easily be proven wrong," Wade said gently.

"No, you'd never want to do that! That would almost be like going to tell a tormented family their missing daughter is dead with zero proof!" Suze snapped.

It was a quiet ride the rest of the way, and they exited the Jeep wordlessly. Wade rang the bell hurriedly, and Deneige answered, showing them in. Wade was once again struck by her appealing looks and shape, but had to focus on the task at hand. He stuffed down any memories of her older sister flashing him and revealing that he meant nothing to her. In a way, it was his first sexual experience, one that stopped as suddenly as it began. Now he was in the presence of a more alluring version of her, kinder, more refined, and sophisticated. She was unintentionally throwing his judgment further off balance than if he'd been struck by a room-sized battering ram.

The St. James family prepared tea and asked Wade what he'd discovered.

"Well, I'm afraid that after having explored all possible avenues of outcomes, we are forced to conclude that Melanie won't be returning home. We feel she has lived out her days and met with foul play," he said.

"How can you be so sure?" Mrs. St. James asked sharply.

"Her purchasing habits stop after a certain date. Her bank card wasn't cancelled over misuse; it was cancelled due to inactivity," Wade said.

"She could have changed banks," her father said.

"We checked; she never changed her name, and if she were operating under an assumed name, she would have cancelled her other digital footprints, including her bank account," Wade said.

"That's not enough to go on; this is our daughter you are talking about. She could have flown to Europe or be hiding from the law with those devil worshippers, waiting for the noise to die down in some cabin out in the woods, or she might be held captive. This is nothing you've given us," he said.

After watching Wade's uncharacteristic behavior of dodging glances and looking at the toes of his shoes, Suzette spoke up.

"Her birth control pills and her prescription ran out before her bank account closed. There were still funds available, and no contact was made to her doctor's office from a new doctor. Unless she was planning a life of celibacy, all these sudden lifestyle departures indicate certain things to us, but I'm afraid we can't tell you the whys and wherefores unless you want to hire for that purpose. But we have scant little to go on, and we just feel you need to be prepared for the worst, as we aren't confident we would have any good news to share. We are so very sorry," Suze said.

"All this charity work is coming from the bottom of your heart, I suppose," Mrs. St. James said, with a cynical scowl.

"What exactly motivates a person to enter your line of work?" Mr. St. James asked.

"Mom, Dad, can't you see it? They are telling you the truth without saying the words because they don't want to hurt you. She's dead. Dead, dead, dead! Look at their faces! They aren't grave diggers. They haven't charged you any money; she's out in the bush somewhere six feet under. You know what kind of people she ran around with. If they find out where her remains are, we could have those very same people taking an interest in us. Read between the lines, damn it," Deneige said.

"Have they ever tried to contact you?" Wade asked.

She didn't answer.

"It's very important; if they are bothering you, we have a little more skill to deal with those types of situations," Suze said.

"So you can't find people, but you think you can stop an organized cult?" Mr. St. James asked.

"Da-ad," Deneige said.

"We can't stop them, but we can demotivate them or encourage them to go elsewhere, often in reduced numbers. If they have records with the police or are thinking of quitting, we can be pretty convincing," Wade said.

"Look, I'll give you my cell number. If you find anything else about them, or Melanie, you can call me. They are called 'Lamashtu's Legion,' and they like to move around quite a bit, probably to distance themselves from their crimes," she said.

Apologies and thanks were exchanged before leaving, and Suze started the Jeep with a quizzical look on her face. Before she could pose any questions, Wade shut the door a little harder than usual.

"They are coming to take her, you know," he said.

"And how exactly would you know that, as a point of fact?" Suzette asked.

"I think she saved someone, and that her life was forfeited as a replacement for whoever she led to safety. So the spared youth to be murdered had to be replaced by Melanie, but then the cult is still one member shy. She may have been a recruiter or even an earner through prostitution or other favors. The cult loses a top recruiter and needs someone to replace her. It has to be someone attractive with charisma who can bring in new members and provide other benefits. Who better than her younger, prettier sister? Who knows what they might do to her to get her to comply? We can't just sit by and let it play out," Wade said.

"So, I can see the accuracy of your crystal ball is in top form, and while you are at it, can you tell me how many we are up against? Where are they situated? What schools did they go to before they got thrown out? The winning number of the next lottery? I mean, you just seem so much more informed than anyone on this case. I just bluffed my ass off and covered for you in there, big time! So cluing me in would be a smart move because I need to know which way the wind blows, and you seem to have a major understanding that everyone else is lacking, and I don't buy into clairvoyance, just for the record," she said.

"Her eyes tilted the wrong way when asked about interference from the cult, and she avoided answering the question entirely. She's seen them parked nearby, following her, sending texts, receiving messages secondhand, or something else," he added.

"Wade, every one of us has our private shit we don't want to be public knowledge, and I'm not going to press you on anything you don't want to share, but have you forgotten this is what we all do, and we can all tell you are more mixed up with this than meets the eye? It's fine, but if there's stuff we need to know, then you need to spill," she said.

"I know they kill people without so much as blinking, and that girl is next in line. I can feel it," Wade said.

"Is there something between you two?" Suze asked.

"What? No! Not in the least, nothing," Wade insisted.

"Uhhhh-huh," Suze agreed patronizingly.

"I said no."

"So she just gave you her cell number when you already had her parents' numbers—a crying out, perhaps, or just an excuse to chat when you guys are alone?"

"You've been watching too many soap operas," he said.

"Wha-at? If she is really at risk, I need to know where her head is at. If they are sophisticated, they could tap her phone, and we'd have all kinds of problems. I don't care if you guys need cuddle time or not. That's none of my business," she said.

"Finally! Suzette respects people's boundaries for the first time. Small miracles! Call the guys and tell them we are going to stake out her place like we did with the old farmer. I'm not dropping the ball on this one."

"Since when do you ever drop the ball?" Suzette asked.

A dune buggy revved up behind them, with two young Asian girls in the back waving their cellphones and taking pictures of them in the Jeep as they passed. A sour look crossed Wade's face as he took notice.

"It's nothing, Wade; you once told me never to let paranoia cloud my judgment, and that was certainly not a family of cult members."

CHAPTER 3

AN EXORBITANT INITIATION FEE

The Pitt reeked of fried food; Angel had made bannock, burgers, and doughy beaver tails that left everyone stuffed full and lazy. The neighboring punks had abandoned their factory dwelling after the arrests, as they had undoubtedly been squatting there illegally. Every person was sprawled across chairs and couches, looking as though they were hungover rather than overfed.

"We're going to have to watch their house, ya know," Jake said, stifling a yawn.

"What do we even know about them, the actual cult? Where do they hang out? How do they recruit? What do they get up to? How do they avoid the cops? What do we know?" Ray asked.

"Lamashtu is just another one of those super creepy characters from demonic mythology that does lots of creepy stuff so brain-dead idiots from our generation can mix and match folklore details to facilitate their sadistic goals. Specifically, she is known for kidnapping infants from breastfeeding women, poisoning water supplies, invading dreams, drinking blood, gnawing on the bones of kids, and all that fun stuff. There is some conflict between the whole bone-gnawing theories and those who believe she transformed the kidnapped into demons or servants, and like in most folklore, there are a lot of gaps. Such gaps allow modern disciples to fill in the blanks with whatever sadistic thing they want to do. She was depicted as a hairy woman on a donkey while suckling a dog and a pig and was known as the rival demon to Pazuzu; in short, a real sweetie," Suzette announced.

"Poisoning a water supply means they drug their victims in modern terms," Stan said.

"They kill people too, and without fear of getting caught, and I don't mean they are clumsy; I wouldn't be shocked to learn that they have some sort of legal protection, or a cop working both sides for them, maybe a fed, a judge, or something. They're very brazen with firearms," Wade said.

"How do you know that?" Angel asked.

"Kidnappers usually want ransom money; these guys grab teenagers and head for the hills. If they were selling them to skin traffickers, Melanie would have been found overdosed, hooking somewhere, or in rehab. If they murder for kicks, it's unlikely they respond well to nosy neighbors or good Samaritans," Wade said.

"I don't doubt your logic, but you seem so sure of all this, almost like you have firsthand knowledge. Have you ever crossed paths with these crazies?" Angel asked.

"Ya seen one, you've seen them all," her boyfriend Jake, said conclusively.

"All I want to know is what we are going to fight them with; if we aren't supposed to use guns and they've got guns, we're back to the chicken-and-egg argument," Stan said.

"Don't start that shit again!" Suzette said, raising her voice.

"We tread carefully, watch them, maybe infiltrate them, catch them at their weakest moment, maybe out of town, and let the cops have 'em where they won't have any clout," Ray said.

"Then how do we join?" Jake asked.

"We watch the St. James house; they've been wanting to get Melanie's sister, but she's on to them and has been hard to isolate. We have to be there when they make the grab."

"…And get shot in the process?" Stan asked.

"They won't need guns to tackle one unarmed single female; suppose we grab one or two of their goons and do a swap for other kids they might be hanging onto," Ray asked.

"Then we'd be the kidnappers," Suzette snapped.

"Then we bring the bats and tattoo them up a bit; maybe teach them not to kidnap and murder people," Ray said.

"Right, and then we wait 'til the rest of them track us down and snipe us one at a time and kill us in our sleep," Jake said.

"We'll have to join and get inside," Stan said.

"What if their entry fee means killing someone?" Ray asked.

"Cults don't usually start up at the top like that, but we don't know with this crew," Jake said.

"Well, while we're here talking about things, Deneige is on her own; I'll take the first watch," Stan said.

About ten hours later, Stan called, asking to be swapped for some sleep. Suzette loaded up on pepper spray and brought extras for Deneige. Days went by, and there were no signs of trouble. The group began to wonder if they'd missed their guess and if the cult had moved on to other regions or found more recruits elsewhere. Concerns were raised over time management, resources, working for free, and safety in general.

Ray followed Deneige into a buy-and-trade music store, pretending to be shopping. A long-haired staff member approached right away.

"Can I help you?" the gaunt man asked Ray.

"No, just looking around; I'll let you know," Ray said.

"Well, you must have something in mind; you look like a guitarist! No? A singer, then? Keys? What's your preference? Maybe you're here to check out the speakers; these ones here are great! Extra bass! And they sound so good, 'cuz they're made out of wood!" he said, beaming a smile as though he'd just quoted Shakespeare's best line.

Deneige had asked about an Airman microphone at the front desk. The female clerk went to check in the back and returned with a well-worn cordless version.

"Eighty bucks," she said.

"That's not a real 'Airman'! Those are rare. It's a knock-off!" a woman of about twenty-five, wearing a hair kerchief and sunglasses, spoke from behind her.

"It's not?" the girl at the desk asked in a surprised tone.

"No, there's no monogrammed clip lock on the side. I've got a real one in my van; I can bring it in here, and I'll sell it to you for fifty," she said.

"You are not allowed to sell goods in our store! See the sign up there?" the clerk reminded her.

"Oh, screw this! You bunch of scammers! Sister, if you want a proper Airman mike for like half of what they're asking, I can put one in your hands right here in thirty seconds," she said.

"Uhmmm, I don't know," Deneige said.

"I understand, but I've got my baby in the van, and I don't want to leave her for too long. You're not afraid of babies, are you?"

"Of course not! Well, it can't hurt to look, right? How old is your daughter?" Deneige asked as the two women exited the store. Ray's assertive salesman was still plying his trade.

"So, if you are not a musician, what are you doing here?" he asked caustically.

"Leaving!" Ray said, taking his two hands and pushing the chest of the salesman out of his path.

He forced his way through the shop doors, only to see the two women approaching the rear of a yellow and brown van.

"Deneige!" he shouted loudly. "You forgot your wedding invitation!"

She turned toward him, confused, muttering, "Wedding invitation?"

She turned again to see a flash of intense anger run across the woman's face for two seconds, her forehead creased above the rims of her sunglasses, yearning for conflict, before quickly yielding a warm grin at Deneige.

"Oops! I forgot! Hubby sold that one already. I'm sorry for wasting your time," she said, still smiling assuringly.

"No worries, thanks anyway," Deneige said.

She then turned to face Ray, looking at him suspiciously.

"What are you doing here? What's this BS about a wedding? Are you following me?" she demanded.

Ray was writing down the license number as the van was already moving into a turn a block ahead.

"Well?" she asked.

"We think the same people your sister got mixed up with might make a play for you, so I stepped in," he said.

"What are you guys? A bunch of professional stalkers or something? Nobody told you to do this! I didn't ask for an escort detail, and no one hired you for that!"

"I know, but…"

"But nothing! What you are doing is creepy."

"Not as creepy as kidnapping. Do you know that woman luring you to the back of a van?"

"She was selling me a mike and showing me her baby!"

"At the back of a van, a woman wants the mike sale done first before she shows her baby, because the baby is bouncing around at the back of a van, not strapped into the passenger seat, correct? Nice of her to stick around and find out about the wedding details, too. All women just hate hearing about weddings and babies, true?"

A long silence followed as Deneige lowered her head and acquiesced. "She looked pretty mad when she saw you, as well," she said.

"And now we have no way to infiltrate the cult, and they've seen me, so we are down by more than a pawn already," Ray said.

"Well, if you guys want in so bloody badly, there's only one thing left to do. If I'm ever going to see the people who murdered my sister, if I'm ever going to get my life back, I'll have to volunteer," Deneige said.

The next day, Suzette and Wade met with her at a diner to prepare her for the daunting task ahead in the hope of dissuading her altogether. They chose a secluded corner and talked over salads and soup.

"Deneige, I'm just not sure if you know how risky this is. Take this flat blade and cut it into the sole of your shoe, if they even let you keep your shoes," Suzette said.

"Then what?"

"If you get the chance to escape and you have to use it, it can cut rope, and in a worst-case scenario, defend yourself," she said.

"In modern combat, most knives are meant for slashing, and that one's too small and flat for much else. If you get cornered alone, slit him across the eyes to mark him and buy yourself time to run. One surprise motion and bolt away without checking for damage, but hopefully it never comes to that. Do your parents know you've made this outrageous decision?" Wade asked.

"Compared to what? Should we wait around like sitting ducks for the next time they decide to terrorize our family? No thanks. Look, we've done everything possible to protect ourselves. We called the cops, all the cult activity hotlines—nothing works against these people," Deneige said.

"That's how they found you! Unless you only call the ones directly affiliated with the authorities, you'll find most of the privately owned ones are actually owned by the larger cults. Think of them as an unintentional snitch line to locate dissenters, angered family members, and other reach-out groups like ours. Did you discuss our involvement?" Wade asked.

"No, it was before that, and they were pretty agreeable about the uselessness of the police, but that seemed legit, and they did ask for a lot of information, like where we lived, and they wanted to know if we had eyes on them or could describe them; that seemed very important to them," she added.

"Instead of you joining them, how about we just let them get a look at you and strike some fear into them?"

"How would I do that? They are the dangerous ones, not me," she said.

"I have a weird idea to bait them, but it's a bit undignified and odd. It depends entirely on how you feel about it, and if you don't want to do it, we'll scrap it and never bring it up again," Wade said.

"I'm listening," she said.

"Well, Suzette here has a sister, and she calls sometimes, and I can never tell their voices apart. They've even fooled her boyfriend, Ray, a few times. In the pictures I've seen, there is a strong resemblance between your sister and yourself; if Suzette played with your hair and we got you some clothes from the secondhand store, do you think you could fool them?" Wade asked cautiously.

"It is a weird idea, but yes, I could pull it off. I don't understand why."

"Do you know any of the cult members' names?" Suzette asked.

"Only from when I was young, there was some guy named 'Ozul,' and he was trying to climb the totem pole and replace his boss or whatever. I think his boss was going by the name of 'Balam' or something like that. They didn't use their real names. Melanie's middle name was Selena, and they changed it to 'Selene'; it's Greek for 'moon,' but in their minds it meant Vampire Queen or something stupid like that," she said.

They drove Deneige home to work on her disguise, visited every dark web listing for sites that offered free personality tests and other cult recruitment tactics to attract new members, and posted a "Dear Balam" notice on every potential cult site imaginable.

Dear Balam:

Will the Vampire Queen sing? I'm back, and I fared far better than your lackeys, but I ramble on too much. I am really trying to reduce the length of my sentences. I kept a journal back in our wild days, and now it holds the key to so many fates. I'd offer it to you, but I don't know that you could afford it. My memory isn't fuzzy. There's no fuzz, but I fear you'd rather face the twisting screw of time than visit me. Should you change your mind, I'll dance at 8 in the abandoned hall this Friday.

Selene

CHAPTER 4

LOCATION, LOCATION, EXECUTION

"Balam, there's a bunch of messages addressed to you all over the dark web," Leila said.

Leila was light-mannered and airy in nature most of the time. She was very attractive, save for the scar that climbed all the way from the tip of her left nostril to just beneath her eye. She had long dark hair, piercing blue eyes, and a mellifluous tone that she could manufacture regardless of her mood. This suited Balam well, as he enjoyed tormenting her and insisted on having her sound pleasant regardless of what state she might be in. He'd carefully taught her to endure physical and psychological pain at intervals of sex or watching others suffer at his hands, so that she might be spared any grief herself. Naturally, she grew to delight in the torment of others and even take part in their suffering to ease her own. She, too, had a dark streak in her persona and was oddly taciturn and indifferent to the experiences of others beyond Balam and herself. Balam had detected a trace of that stark coldness within her and cultivated it masterfully, so that now she remained partly his plaything and partly his unpaid employee, whose title might have been the henchman's apprentice.

Balam, or Maurice Hope, as he was christened, had reached his position in life by seeking a position of advantage over anyone he could. It was a classic tale. When he acted out in vile ways and the other children noticed or took exception, his bark was worse than his bite. Most of the fights he started he was unable to finish, and often he was beaten up, usually over his disturbing commentary. He wanted very much to be victorious, but unlike most kids who lose a fight or two, he was unwilling to put the work in by learning a combat sport or increasing his strength with weights. Instead, he began to look for more helpless victims: a neighbor's pet, a girl half his age and size, an injured person crawling away from an accident. Like many disturbed criminals, he began with rodents and rabbits, and he worked his way up to larger prey, often using weapons like knives as his instruments or ropes to limit breathing and extend torment as long as possible. The more people noticed his distaste for others, the more they avoided him. This resolved nothing, as it only meant there were fewer around to detect his growing anti-human tendencies. If everyone avoided him, that suited Balam best because it meant there was no one to supervise him or chaperone him. His kindly grandmother had sight and hearing limitations, and her compassionate behavior only irked him. He inherited her house and a fair sum after her death, when he was only eighteen years old. He'd cringe whenever people complimented or commented on his last name and its meaning, and he decided he'd live his life with the purpose of taking hope away from people rather than restoring it. He soon learned that in order to manipulate people, it was imperative to fill them with false hope, and then his satisfaction would be far greater, as their emotional crash-landing into fear was always more drastic when they fell fast from a great emotional height.

At this moment, Balam's own emotions were squirming to find a comfortable place as he read this unlikely message.

"It's cryptic," Leila said.

"Not really; she's got some dirt on me and wants something—money, to put me away, or something worse. I need to find out what she's up to," he said.

"Who?"

"Never mind! Here, take this burner phone, and I'll get you a number. Ask for Selene. No, Selena. No, wait a minute, Melanie! Just ask if she's there; if they act baffled, hang up. If she's there, find out what the hell she wants, OK?"

Deneige closed the fall board of her piano, unable to focus on anything melodic, when the phone rang.

"Hello, is Melanie there?" a female voice asked.

A cold chill ran over Deneige's entire body as she tried to restrain her eyes from bulging. Melanie had long been missing, presumed dead, and the coldness and nonchalance of the voice asking seemed as though it, too, might as well be from beyond the grave. Deneige was caught off guard by the call coming so swiftly after Suzette had only mentioned planning to send out a message and not expecting any response for a few days.

"No," Deneige said.

"Okay, never mind," the voice said.

"She's in the shower. Oh, wait, she's coming out now. Hold on a second," Deneige said.

She then placed the phone on the pillow and called Suzette.

"A woman called looking for Melanie; I said she's in the shower! What now?" she asked.

"Do an impression of your sister by acting all cocky, like she has them by the bag, and taunt them! Can you do that?" Suzette asked.

"I think so," she said, construing her facial expression to that of her deceased sister's.

"I'll get Wade, and we'll listen in. Put her on speaker so we can hear, OK?"

"Hello. Whatcha want?" Deneige asked brusquely.

"So, you're back, are you?" a female voice started but was taken over by an aggressive male voice without warning.

"—Give me that! I'll take it from here! … This is Balam. What the fuck are you up to? Everyone says you're dead! No sign of you for years, and now you show up out of the blue looking for a shakedown. Are you out of your mind? Do you know what could happen if you play this wrong? You'll be feeding the crows from your eye sockets if you screw me over! Get the picture, Selene?"

"Oh, you guys with your little peckers, always barking like little dogs until the fence opens, and then your tails drop between your legs and ya start yelping. You sound scared, and ya should be. I've been talking to this fed, real high up, and I can skirt all my charges if I toss you into his salad. All he wants is my booklet, an' he says it's enough. I've dodged him for years, though; that's why you haven't heard from me. I had to keep it on the down-low, but now he wants to drop everything against me and get you. So I want to know what it's worth to you. My silence and my little bookie-wookie? Huh? Whatcha got fer me?"

"What's that echo? Am I on speakerphone? Are you recording this?" Balam roared.

"Men are so dumb. I can't record myself blackmailing you, Lamebrain! I want ten grand on Friday at eight! No show or play rough, and it goes to the feds unless I cancel the courier, so better hit the bank! Tah-tah!" Deneige said as she hung up.

"Okay, I hung up; he was freaking me out," she said with a long exhalation.

"That was fantastic! You really sounded just like… a completely different person," Wade said.

"I did some acting in school," Deneige said.

"Well, you were terrific!" Suzette said, reclaiming her phone.

"What now?"

"You stay home for a few days; we'll be watching the house, then a cameo on Friday, and we'll see what's what. You did great!" Suzette said.

Suzette turned and faced Wade with a concerned stare.

"What happens if they show up at her place with guns?"

"They won't! Jake's watching the house, so I want you and Angel to go to the army surplus store and pick up some black rent-a-cop uniforms, and I'll bring the guns," Wade said.

"Guns? I thought only Jake had the key, and what about their uniform sizes? I thought we weren't going to ever use guns! That's what you said," Suzette said.

"You're a girl! You'll guess everyone's size better than anyone else, and I only have a spare gun key in case anything happens to Jake; he wanted it like that," Wade said.

For the next two days, Ray and Stan fired pistols at bottles and cans on the front lawn of St. James's home for display, as there was little doubt the house was being watched. When they grew tired, Wade and Jake took over, always in face-obscuring riot helmets. Mr. and Mrs. St. James didn't favor the idea, but Deneige convinced them, and they seemed too fatigued to refute it much.

Friday came fast, and the abandoned hall Suzette referred to was a boarded-up movie theater the cult had squatted in years ago before they'd gained stability. Suzette and Deneige watched the news as several channels were covering a rash of liquor store robberies that had occurred across the city at many different locations.

"Remember, if they call, accuse them of not having the money and hang up," Suzette said.

The old theater stood tall at three stories and had a large double entrance with a small foyer that led to a grand stage surrounded by upper balconies and a catwalk that encompassed the whole interior. Outside, there were clusters of light bulbs that formed letters for shining displays. Most of the bulbs were broken, and the main sign had begun to sag and surrender to chipped paint and general decay. There were two outside balconies that could showcase headliners if they wanted to wave at the incoming crowds. The east balcony hadn't been opened in years, and the door locks were rusted shut. The west, however, was missing its door, and there was Deneige in tight faded jeans and a loose-fitting white blouse tied across her midriff, exposing her navel. She wore sunglasses and left her hair out and a bit unkempt. Wade was struck by the uncanny image, as he'd have sworn Melanie had returned from the grave. Stan and Ray had finished mounting the speakers and camouflaging them on either side of the theater's exterior.

Two cars approached slowly: an Impala and a full-sized van. Before they stopped, a phone call came in.

"So, where's the book? You better have it, and how do I know you didn't make copies?" Balam asked.

"It's my journal, Jackass! There's a lot of stuff I don't want the narcs to know I did either. Are you completely brain-dead? You got the money?" Deneige asked.

"Yeah, we got it," Balam grunted.

"Bullshit! You couldn't scrape it up that fast. Where'd you get that kinda cash? Tell me now or I split," Deneige said.

"Well, maybe Dark Rum pirates helped me out. Now where is it?" Balam asked.

"Up here!" Deneige stepped out from behind a curtain on the outer balcony and waved a recipe book at them before ducking right back in. She remembered the liquor store robbers had used Uzis and realized the cult might have the money after all. There was an old fire escape pole beside the stairwell, and she slid down it in seconds and ran out the back way to Suzette, who was waiting in the Jeep with the engine already running. Three men and a woman got out of the cars, and they were carrying Uzis. Two spread out, and two entered the building as Stan and Ray took out their nail guns, fired at the tires of both vehicles, and ran for the unused security side entrance. Once inside, Stan heard some bullet spray rattling across the door as he locked it behind him. Ray found a stairwell to the basement and stowed himself away in the dark.

Halfway to the highway, another call came in, and Deneige answered.

"Where the fuck is the book?" Balam demanded.

Deneige answered in her own voice.

"I don't know what you are talking about. You are the guys who killed my sister, and I fingered you to the cops. Now they're on their way! I sure hope you like jail food!"

Wade was on the roof and signaled Jake to start the siren, which blasted into a public address system, and the outdoor speakers amplified the sound to a deafening level. This was done to panic the cultists, partly due to concerns over the police arriving late.

The two drivers exited their vehicles, examining their tire damage, and started to run as the remaining cultists scattered from the theater in all directions. When the police finally arrived, they found a note clipped under a windshield wiper on the van.

Dear Police: Please examine the contents of this vehicle. We're confident you'll find money from recent liquor store robberies, and if you trace the owners of the vehicles, you'll find a history of abductions and murders. Just ask Maurice Hope and Leila Van Koenig. They are responsible for the deaths of Melanie St. James and others. If he won't confess, she might. Good luck!

Suzette dropped Deneige off at her parents' home, gave her a hug at the door, and turned back toward the Jeep.

"Aren't you going to come in?" Deneige asked.

"Naw, you need time with your family, and honestly speaking, we're kind of outsiders to most people, and given our line of work, it's probably best that way," Suzette said.

"Right, but after all you've done, I'm sure my folks will want to compensate you in some manner and at least give you their thanks," Deneige said, smiling.

"Wade thinks your family has been through enough as it is, and there is no guarantee things won't crop up ten years down the road, so he won't take a cent, and he's adamant about it. It's funny; usually he's the stickler over money, and now he won't hear a word about it. Give my best to your folks," Suzette said.

"Can I have his number? Maybe I can change his mind," Deneige asked.

"Just call the office; we all get our messages there," Suzette said before driving off.

The next day, a police cruiser arrived at the St. James home, and two officers rang the bell.

They questioned the St. James family about Melanie and the shootout at the theater, but the parents were oblivious, and because the cultists were certain it was the deceased Melanie they'd seen at the theater, there was no backlash pointed at Deneige. They inquired about the rent-a-cops seen out front of the St. James residence, and the faces of the St. James family collectively soured all at once.

"We didn't hire them; in fact, the only people we contacted were from the Cult Activity Hotline, so we just assumed they sent them. I think that's what they said. You should really talk to them. They seem to have all kinds of information about which cults are doing what and where they are located. I'm certain they'd be very eager to share any information you might need. We didn't ask for names or badge numbers; we just thought they were here to protect us, so we said 'fine,'" Deneige added.

The more senior policeman asked, "So some guys in uniforms with guns show up and you don't even ask for identification?"

"No, and now that you mention it, we didn't ask you for yours either. May I know your names and badge numbers?" Deneige asked.

The police provided their information and left their business cards as well. They politely left a few minutes later, looking marginally dissatisfied with their unproductive interviews.

Back at The Pitt, Angel was serving up drinks to everyone, but Jake only watched as rock music blasted with drunken imitations of the stunned cultists as the police explained that their accused blackmailer was a dead person. They reimagined Balam blaming blackmail on a murder victim he was resposible for. Stan imitated Ray stumbling in the dark, trying to avoid gunfire, knocking things over loudly, and then saying, "Uh-oh." Jake impersonated the van driver, trying to run away but wanting to check his tires while at the same time stuck in a state of cognitive dissonance. Ray performed as the reimagined cult leader, explaining to his lawyer that they were set up by a corpse.

"Melanie St. James! She's behind all this! Ask her!" Ray shouted.

"You know she's dead, right?" Angel joined in, feigning an authoritative voice.

"Who killed her?"

"You did! Eight years ago!" Angel snapped, and everyone laughed heartily.

"Hey! Where's Wade?" Jake asked.

"Up in his room," Stan said.

"He should be here with us; he did a lot on this one," Angel said.

"I don't know, he seemed a bit thrown off the whole time. Maybe we should just leave him alone; he knows we're down here," Suzette said.

"I'll go talk to him," Jake said.

"Tell him little Miss 'White as the Driven Snow' asked for his number; maybe that'll put a smile on his face," Suzette said, smirking.

Wade emerged at the top of the stairs and smiled at the group.

"Sorry, guys, I just want to tell you all how proud I am of each and every one of you. This was a tough one. They had Uzis, and that's a fair bit beyond our pay grade. We risked our lives, and everybody answered the bell like champs. You guys were brilliant, but Riley's been darting back and forth across the window and making this weird whimpering noise at me every few minutes. It took me a while to notice, but there is a car two lots down the road with lights off, and there are two guys in it that have been watching our place for hours," he said.

"So they need to be drawn out by someone they've never met before, and I've been cooped up in here cooking, taking calls, and leading the quiet life. It's time I did something more concrete!" Angel said.

"Now hold on a sec there," Jake said.

"If you should go, they'll be aggressive and react to your height; Stan's too scary-looking, and they're probably watching for Ray, Suze, or Wade, so it has to be me," Angel insisted.

Twenty minutes later, Angel approached the tan Kia Optima on foot, swaying her body in the shortest mini skirt she had. She shuffled as she walked, intermittently humming a song and then botching some lyrics.

"Hey, those guys stole my bike! Officers, those guys stole my bike!" She shouted.

The two men in the car did not react, so Angel grew more brazen.

"Oh, so you don't care if a Native gets their bike stolen; you only care if it's a white person, right?"

The driver gave her a sideward glance that spoke more of fatigue and disinterest rather than the irritation she was seeking.

"Racist cops! Racist cops, right here in the neighborhood!" she shouted loudly.

"We're not cops!" the driver snapped.

"Then what're yas all doin' here? Ohhh, I get it, you're lookin' for a lil action, an' ya brought a friend 'cuz you're shy, I gotcha," she said.

The two men in suits and ties after hours remained steadfast and silent, refusing to take Angel's bait.

"Oh, you think I won't play ball? Is that it? I'll letchyas see my cootchie for ten bones. I'm just tryin' to get enough for cab fare home," she said.

"Not interested," the voice from the passenger seat said.

"Oh, it's like that, is it? You're peeping Toms! Hey everyone, we got peeping Toms right here, watchin' yas all through their car windows," she shouted.

She heard the sound of a key turning over the ignition as the headlights lit up and the Kia drove off. Angel returned to The Pitt with a mini-debriefing.

"Well, they weren't cops; they had no radio in the car. They didn't seem to care that I was acting like I was on crack or soliciting. They didn't act defensive about being called racists or peeping Toms, for that matter," she said.

"Feds?" Stan asked.

"Maybe, but they looked more like corporate heavies or private agency types. They were very disciplined and low-key, but they sure didn't like being noticed. I'll tell you that much," she added.

"Looks?" Suze asked.

"Average enough, fit, I didn't see any shoulder holsters, not as far as I could tell. Their hair was short enough but not military or law; they were clean-shaven, and they were on the bigger side; that's about it," Angel said, with a shrug.

The following day, Wade went to the bank for a withdrawal to help compensate for not charging the St. James family any fees, and he felt he should provide some additional funds for the food budget. As he withdrew his cash, he noticed a man observing him, and he had two others in suits close behind him.

"Mr. Axtol?" the well-dressed man with brown hair asked politely.

"I think you've made a mistake," Wade said.

"Oh, I don't think so. You see, my name is Balcom. I'm sort of what you might call a fixer; when people have problems, they call me. They might be stuck in a jam, have legal problems, or even have problems with the authorities. When they do call me, it's because they know there is almost no problem I can't fix. Now, wouldn't it be nice to have a friend like that, just in case you ever ran into a problem? Here's my card. I think it's important that you don't lose it. You can never tell when you might run into some difficulty and need someone to represent you or negotiate for you, just in case! Oh, and Mr. Axtol, I don't make mistakes," he added.

"You've misunderstood me, I'm afraid. I didn't mean you got my name wrong; I meant following me to a bank and then wasting my time with your slimy spiel, thinking you get to keep your teeth. That seems like a horrendous miscalculation to me. Are you looking for some free dentistry because you have too many teeth in your mouth? Or because your mouth is too big? I really can't tell," Wade said coolly.

"I'm no enemy of yours; if anything, I think you'd find knowing me could be quite the anodyne to any struggles you might endure now or in the future. Call if you change your mind, and I might recommend trying herbal tea; it helps keep those stress levels down," Balcom said before rejoining his two smirking bodyguards.

"Do you know what they say about free advice, Balcom?"

"No, what do they say?"

"It's usually worth exactly what you paid for it," Wade said, scowling.

Balcom nodded and waved condescendingly as he left. Wade walked to his rendezvous point, examining the business card with just a name and phone number that read "Emerson Balcom" and no job title. Shortly afterward, Jake came around the corner in the Jeep and opened the passenger door just minutes before they were supposed to meet. Jake tossed a phone to Wade.

"It's for you," he said.

He took Suzette's phone and heard Deneige's voice.

"Wade! Oh my word, there are some people here from the government, and they are really leaning hard on my parents, and I don't know what to do," she said.

"Tell them you've discovered the Lord, and then redirect every single question back to God's work and right vs. wrong morality. If they get heavy with you, tell them that cults do ungodly things all the time. Then ask if they are doing ungodly things, just like the cult, by getting so pushy; they'll hate that. If they don't ease up, get out your Bible, start talking about Daniel and the lions, and read them actual verses to prove your case. If they are legit, they will pack up and leave in order to allocate their time more wisely. If not, don't worry, we are on our way!" he said.

CHAPTER 5

⊕FFER DECLINED

ake and Wade pulled up to the St. James residence only to notice three men in business attire exiting via the front door.

"Jake, can you follow them without being noticed? They're probably well-trained at spotting a tail. It won't be easy; I'll check in on the family and find out what they told them," Wade said.

"I'll have to hang way back, and it'll be tricky, but I can handle it," Jake said.

Mrs. St. James opened the door and welcomed him in.

"What did those men want? What exactly did they say? Who specifically do they work for?" Wade asked impatiently.

"They said they were from the government and the something-something branch; it was long government-speak. They flashed their IDs at us, but I only had time to check if the photos matched. One name was Sanford, he was in charge, and they were all special investigator this and special agent that. They were very special, I suppose," she said.

"What'd they want?"

"They asked a lot of questions, so we just kept telling them what we already told the police and told them to check with them," she said.

"They pressed us on when we last saw Melanie and where," Mr. St. James said, straightening his glasses.

"Unprofessional?" Wade asked.

"Not really, but they did quasi-threaten us about knowing more than we were letting on. It was only when Deneige started Bible-thumping them that they got annoyed and moved on," Mr. St. James said.

"Did they leave a card?"

"Yes, Deneige has it up in her room; you can go check with her," he said.

"Hi, Deneige, do you have a card from those guys?"

"Yes, thanks for coming; they said they were from Ameripol, but when I call the listed numbers, I only get answering machines and recordings to call other numbers. It sure would be a good front if they're faking," she said.

"Well, it is the weekend, and Ameripol is supposed to be a sort of grand liaison of police forces and can probably hop jurisdictions with ease, so let's not jump the gun until we know what's what; besides, if you were trying to fool people, they would've just said FBI or whatever," Wade said.

"I asked Suze for your number, with everything that's going on, but she wouldn't disclose it for security reasons, I guess," Deneige said.

"It's not that; I just hate cell phones with a passion. Have you ever been on a date and the person kept checking their phone? I just walk away while they take their calls," Wade said.

"I wouldn't know," Deneige said.

"About which part?"

"About dating, I never did it much," she said.

"*You've* never dated much? How come?" Wade asked, restraining his eyes from bulging.

"When your sister runs off with a cult, your parents get protective, and when I did find that one guy I liked, he liked me back, but he liked drugs better," Deneige said.

"One guy? I mean, no disrespect, but girls who look like you aren't usually restricted to the attention of just one guy, from what I can tell," Wade said.

"Guys think I'm an egghead: music, dance, theater, high marks in school. Now I'm doing university through correspondence so Mum 'n' Dad can keep an eye on me, but it gets tedious at times, ya know?" she asked.

"I had no idea; I'm sorry," Wade said.

"Oh, it's okay; I have the Internet and seventeenth-century poetry to keep me company," she said with a giggle.

"Well, I am no expert, but you look more of the Lady Mary Wroth type than an Anne Locke fan to me, but I never even went to high school, so I probably don't know what I am talking about," he said.

"Get out of here! You discovered those authors on your own?" she asked incredulously.

"I cleaned up after horses for a lady with a big book collection," he said.

"You must tell me more about this," she insisted.

"I should go. Your folks, the case, Jake's probably waiting for me. May I use your phone?"

It rang just before she handed it to him, and it was Sanford. She answered and put the phone between Wade and herself so he could hear.

"Ms. St. James, I heard you'd been calling us, and I want you to feel free to use my direct line. What I want to know is if you'd be willing to provide a DNA sample so that we can eliminate some 'Jane Does' from the search for your sister," Sanford said.

She turned to face Wade, and he nodded.

"Yes, it's fine. When will that be?" Deneige asked.

"I'll send someone tomorrow at 11:00 AM. Is that alright?"

"Fine, goodbye," she said and hung up.

Wade dialed Jake, who confirmed the men he followed were leaving the state, and he would be back in twenty minutes to pick Wade up.

"I have to go wait for Jake," Wade said.

"It sounded like he said twenty minutes; he's got a big enough voice so I could hear. Will you wait on the front lawn then?" she asked.

"I, um, don't like to be anything less than professional in my work, sort of like not mixing business with pleasure," Wade said.

"It's not business! You never charged us anything, remember? What's the issue here? Do I make you uncomfortable or something?" Deneige asked.

"Look, you are going to be a world leader or something, and I'm just a guy who barely escaped skid row. I think you are an outstanding individual, and I feel graced to have met you, but I am miles out of my element here, and I have no illusions about it. You can see that, right?" he asked.

"That's reverse elitism you're engaging in, you know," she countered.

"Is it?"

"Sure, it's like a guy from the hood makes good and goes to England and has a one-night stand with a daughter of the Royal family, but he fears he'll never fit in or be accepted, so he subjects the girl to the very same barriers he imagines he's facing and makes them even more impenetrable by telling her he can't see her again because he has to go back to his hayseed liquor shack out back, even though he doesn't have one. Now he's free from having to fit in, and any fears of intimacy and not being good enough are shut down. As long as she's not pregnant, it was a shiny day for him, except for the fact that he wanted more than that and convinced himself otherwise. By cowering from his feelings, he's left alone, wondering 'what if' for the rest of his days. With a touch more courage and dropping the pretense that class distinction rules all, he probably could have had all he wanted," she said.

"Maybe he just didn't care for the scones and crumpets," Wade said.

"I think you are hiding behind this cheap camouflage of pithy rationale and cheap banter; I think you've got the fever for me, and you're just too scared to admit it," Deneige charged.

"Well, who wouldn't have the bloody fever for you? Look at you! You're like a living statue hand-carved by the gods. I'd be surprised if every security cam on this street wasn't pointed at your house all day," Wade said defensively.

"So you think I look old, then?" Deneige asked.

"Comical," he countered.

They looked at each other as the seconds passed until the tension in the air was so thick it had to be broken. Wade then took her in his arms and kissed her like only a man who'd been without female affection for months could. He'd stopped tracking all the bad ideas he was allowing to run amok on this case, as part of him wondered whether he'd lost his mind entirely.

Jake honked the horn, and Wade strode up to the Jeep quickly. Upon entering, he pulled the passenger seat back and propped his feet up on the dashboard, looking like he wanted to sleep.

"Ohhhh-Kay," Jake said, looking at Wade's stretched-out form with a perplexed expression.

"Don't worry," Wade grunted.

"This isn't going to be one of those 'It all started with my childhood' kind of conversations, is it?" Jake asked, frowning.

"Have I ever done that?" Wade asked.

"Well, it's just that I don't usually save my shrink's couch for road trips. Now, what's going on with you? Everyone says you're acting funny, and I keep saying you're fine. Now you're acting like you need to get your blood checked or something. What gives?" Jake asked.

"Everything's fine."

"You haven't been eating too many of those sugary cereals from back in the day, have ya?"

"Never. I'm fine, Mr. E.Q. regulator," Wade said.

"I smell perfume," Jake said.

"Really?" Wade asked.

"You didn't! Oh my God, you did! You did! In there? While her parents were home? I mean, it wasn't with the mother, was it? Oh my

God, I can't believe you! I thought you'd been working too hard lately; I didn't know you were working on your game. That's why you've been acting so nuts; it's the chick!" Jake exhorted loudly.

"No. I didn't. I just, well, you know, we had a little moment. It was nothing."

"Well, as long as you didn't corrupt her DNA sample for tomorrow! As a motherfuckin' professional, that's all I care about. Sorry, I didn't mean anything toward the mother. I mean, if there was any surprise DNA contamination of some kind, that would be a tricky thing to have to explain, right? Living on the razor wire much, these days?"

"Are you done?" Wade asked.

"No, sir, I was not the one getting done, being done, or done over. I'm just the poor sap trying to make sure we stay on top of our game. Well, okay, not that kinda game, but clean living and not mixing the client's sugar in with the company coffee, that's me. I get to be the dutiful and responsible one for a change. I kind of like the ring to that, to tell you the truth," Jake said, unable to contain his laughter.

"Maybe we should print you a t-shirt that reads, 'I never bent the rules.'"

"Let's not go too far!" Jake said, pretending to be offended.

Jake's phone rang, and it was Deneige.

"Here, it's for you, and it didn't take very long, did it?" Jake asked with a knowing grin.

"Wade, it's me; they've found my sister's remains way up north in Ridgebreak Falls. Do you know where that is?" Deneige asked.

Wade immediately sat up straight, rigid as a board, and listened intently.

"Just tell me what happened," he said.

CHAPTER 6

WOUNDED PRIDE

Suzette finished her research early and left the library, pleased with her results. She had written Monica, a former client, a letter in hopes that it might clear up any misunderstanding about her wanting to become better friends, but she had been ghosted by her and never understood why. She would be meeting Ray after his sparring session at the gym and decided to stop at a patio bar to touch up her letter so that there could be no doubt about her honest intentions. She ordered a virgin Caesar, retouched a few lines, and placed the paper, along with a friendship card, in an envelope and sealed it.

A group of attractive girls in their early twenties came walking along the sidewalk carrying takeout food and drinks, looked directly at Suzette through their sunglasses, and stopped at the edge of the sidewalk closest to her table. Suzette smiled, wondering if they'd mistaken her for someone else.

"Yeah, that's her!" a pretty redhead said to her blonde friend, while two others nodded in agreement.

Suzette smiled again and tilted her head slightly, eager to rectify the confusion.

"That chick is a ho!" the blonde shouted.

"What?" Suzette asked, shaking her head and blinking repeatedly.

"She's a whore!" the assertive blonde shouted even louder.

"A homewrecker! She slept with my man while I was pregnant, and we just had a baby!" the redhead, sporting a kerchief as a head cover, confirmed.

"Look, I don't even know you people!" Suzette said indignantly.

The blonde pulled out her cell phone and played a video clip of a girl looking similar to Suzette seducing a reluctant man. Suzette rushed to the phone and was startled at the resemblance of the woman in the video doing shady things to a man who kept pulling away from her.

"That's not me!" Suzette said, raising her voice.

One by one, the girls started showing all the customers the video from each of their phones and asking their opinions if it was indeed her. All of the people viewing the videos turned their eyes to Suzette in judgment. Even the waitress could be seen nodding and then frowning. Suzette turned, looking at all the reactions, as within minutes these girls had turned the entire patio crowd against her. Suzette cursed herself for not recognizing the setup sooner. She knew she had to exit the scene for safety's sake, but she didn't want to leave before knowing who her assailants were.

"Don't you look at me, you cheap whore!"

The redhead screamed at her. She then opened the contents of her takeout, which included black bean soup, and poured it down Suzette's white blouse. Suzette stood up in shock at the mess as the blonde, in turn, pelted her with a plastic cup full of cola.

"Better watch your step, bitch," a third girl with long black hair growled through a vengeful glare just before they left. The four piled into a blue Mazda and sped off, cackling wildly.

Suze had a lot of courage and a penchant for daring acts, but she didn't do well with humiliation. The clientele all stared at her, with a few pretending not to, as she fought back tears—not from feeling defeated or bullied, but from feeling so completely alone among a crowd of people without a single person defending her.

Jake arrived at the gym to pick up Ray, and as was his custom, he stopped in to watch the sparring and give Ray his unsolicited opinions on Ray's tactics and methods. After changing, Ray came out to Jake, swearing loudly and at length as he noticed two of the Jeep's tires had been slashed, and they only had one spare. This meant Ray'd be late for Suzette, and she always hated it whenever he was late.

He called Suzette.

"Hey, it's me. Sorry, but it looks like I'm gonna be late," he said.

"Of course," she said.

"Hey, don't be like that. You haven't even heard what happened yet," Ray said.

"Doesn't matter. I'll see you back at The Pitt," Suzette said and hung up.

Angel went to the farmer's market to pick up some ingredients, as Wade had given her some extra funds as a bonus for not throwing cutlery at them when they didn't finish their plates.

As she went to pay for her groceries, a girl with long black hair shouted at the farmer.

"I forgot to tip you before!"

She came running up to the cash area and, in one slick and subtle move, pried Angel's bank card out of her hand and passed it to a blonde girl who ran and then passed it to another, but Angel wasn't having it.

She ran and leaped onto the black-haired girl's back and curled her left arm around the girl's neck, and with her right hand, she grabbed a pop bottle and broke the end off by smashing it against a table.

"If you don't get my bank card back, I'll cut your pretty little face off, right here, right now," she said, lightly pressing the bottle to her neck.

"C.J., quick! She's got me! Give it back!" the girl shrieked.

After a few seconds with neither side blinking, people started taking out their phones, and Angel had no desire to become an internet star. She immediately let go and quickly tossed the bottle in a waste container.

"I'll report it stolen and get another one. I don't even care," Angel said.

A girl with red hair in a kerchief and sunglasses flicked her wrist and sent the card spinning into the air, the way one might flick a playing card to watch it sail across a room. Out into the traffic it went, but Angel didn't follow it. She wasn't sure what game was afoot, but she knew she didn't want to be the donkey for someone to pin a tail on.

That evening, Stan found himself across town in a strip bar called Lacey's Nook, where he was trying to endear himself to a dancer known as Tasha. He wanted to be sure she could hear him away from the noise and bustle, so he was biding his time and indulging in repeated shots of straight vodka. As customers began to fill up the seating area, a man of average height and build asked Stan if he could share his table. Stan motioned his hand toward an empty seat and said nothing. The man was in a suit; he had gray-blue eyes, brown hair, and a mustache.

"Buy you a drink?" the man asked.

"Nah, I'm fine," Stan replied.

"Oh, well, it's just that I got a bonus from work this week, and you were good enough to let me share your table, so I thought I'd repay the favor," he said.

"It's your money," Stan said.

"Sure, I'm happy to; besides, you look like a pretty rugged guy, a bit rough and tumble. That's cool, but I'm not like that, so I don't want to get on anybody's bad side," the stranger said.

The waitress brought a beer and another vodka for Stan, who rarely appeared drunk until consciousness faltered, and tonight he'd been well overserved.

"You hold your water pretty good," his table guest said, as the waitress collected the glasses Stan had emptied.

"I expect you are leading up to a specific point in this conversation; what is it?" Stan muttered.

"Oh, I'm just making conversation; I'm not looking to make any long-term friends. Don't worry! It's just, uh, that you are pretty wide across and look like you can handle yourself, so I was wondering if you were a martial arts guy, like an MMA fighter or something like that, that's all," he said.

"I had a price dispute with a lady in a grocery store once," Stan said.

"Well, I hope you came out on top. You know, I've always admired the tough guys. If you take that big guy over there, I bet you can't guess his weight; I'd put him at six foot seven and two hundred and eighty pounds. That's one hefty dude. If you look over at the bar, you'll see a giant black guy, and I say he's six foot five and two-sixty, all solid muscle. People probably think they're the bouncers here or football players on their day off, but I don't think so. Would you like to make a friendly wager?" the stranger asked. Stan had noticed them when he came in and did take them for bouncers, but got distracted by Tasha's movements and paid them little attention.

"I don't care what anybody weighs. If you're so taken with them, go ask," Stan said with a sour shrug.

"I don't have to ask them because I know them. The ripped guy in the black T-shirt, that's Tony, and the black behemoth in suspenders over there, he's Greg. Now, those are two guys nobody in their right mind would want to tangle with, that's for sure. They'd make minced meat out of any gym rat or local street tough with a chip on his shoulder, wouldn't you think?"

"Well, before you go ask for their autographs, I wouldn't hand out the hero biscuits just yet. Tony favors one leg ever so slightly; that's a lot of stress on the knees when you roid out like that, and Greg has bulky thighs, which means he can't be too fast or agile on his feet, just saying," Stan said.

"Nah, you don't get it; these guys are bigger than the bouncers, and if things ever got ugly, I don't even think those low-budget bouncers would even try to stop them. Betcha they wouldn't say shit and would pretend they never saw a thing. How's about I call them both over here, and you can tell them about how weak-kneed and slow you think they are? Hey, Greg! Tony! Come have a drink with us!" the stranger said with a malicious grin. The two large men came and sat close enough to Stan that they were imposing on his personal space.

"This guy here thinks neither one of you could fight your way out of a paper bag. He says you walk funny, and you look slower than the Brazilian economy. Greg is half-Brazilian, just to let you know," the table guest said, grinning.

Stan leaned back in his chair, placed his hands behind his back, and fished around for the wooden slats in the backrest of his chair. In one sudden motion, he snapped off a slat from the chair and used it as a choking bar across Tony's neck. As Tony attempted to grab Stan with his formidable arms, Stan stomped him on the side of his weaker knee and brought him to the ground. He then lifted Tony's head, still choking him with the slat, and stood on the back of his calf, preventing him from getting up as the muscleman's face reddened and began to swell, while Stan swung him around like a shield to block Greg's advances.

"You want me to kill him? Keep coming!" Stan said.

Tony's eyes were widening, the veins in his neck bulged, and he was gurgling up spittle as he struggled to suck in air.

"You want him dead? It'll be on your hands," Stan reminded Greg as he swung Tony into Greg's path a second time, as Tony desperately tried to wheeze in air.

Greg's eyes were bulging too, only with rage.

"You think I'm going to let you walk?" Greg snorted.

"You're right," Stan said, as he began dragging Tony backward, the slat embedding deeper into his neck. Tony clumsily tried to maintain his balance while being dragged backward toward the door.

Just before exiting, Stan noticed the man who bought him the drink sneaking out the back way. Then he rammed the strong man's forehead into the wall dazing him, as Tony was already short of breath. While his body collapsed to the ground, Stan twisted away from him and threw the slat at Greg's face.

Greg rushed him, and Stan leaped out of his path.

"I'll see you again, one on one, Greggy," Stan said.

Greg chased after Stan out into a side street, but after about thirty yards, he slowed and had to catch his breath.

"What's the matter? Can't keep up? Outta shape? Want me to run slower?" Stan jeered, and once again, Greg angrily pursued.

This went on only for another twenty paces, and Greg again slowed to a stop, breathing heavily.

Stan came running toward Greg and leaped in the air, kicking him in the chest as both men tumbled to the ground. Stan clutched his hair, pulling it upward, and kneed him in the face repeatedly, switching knees until Greg toppled over and raised his hands in defeat. Stan kicked him in the face, and grabbed an ankle as her fell. The twist and snap were immediate but the sweat covered, half-Brazillian only shut his eyes tight and grimaced.

"Until next time, Greggy!" Stan said, as he ran off, never to see Tasha again.

Back at The Pitt, Wade was pacing back and forth, and Riley was following him like it was a new game because he hadn't seen it before. One by one, each person came in, either slamming doors, swearing, or throwing their jackets across the room as they entered. Only Stan was composed, but didn't look happy.

As each took their turn reiterating the day's events they faced, each grew more concerned over the scope of what they were collectively up against.

"Maybe we should just quit; it's been a wild run, but we're getting out of our elememt here. We're facing people with Uzis, seasoned con men, hired muscle, female blackmailers, and probably organized crime next. We're getting into mob-style pissing contests, and we don't have enough chips to cover the entance fee. We're not even sure who's holding the cards while they rattle our chains. This was supposed to be about freeing people from cults, but now it's turned into this seedy world of dark crime and having to learn who Ameripol is. We are out of our league, and people are putting nooses around our necks, probably prices on our heads, and all for what? We help some dead girl's family, who aren't even paying us. We've taken a very wrong turn, and we may never get our lives in order again and might all end up dead! Someone tell me I'm wrong here; I'm waiting!" Suzette said.

"That's how they want us to feel," Ray said.

"Well, it's working, Ray! I feel like shit, and I'm scared shitless, and angry. I don't want to live like this, so it's mission accomplished for them!" Suzette rebutted.

The room fell silent for a few minutes, and Riley sat next to Suzette to comfort her. Facial expressions softened as anger gave way to concern for Suzette. She had no real female friends to speak of, and Ray had been through some tough scraps recently, both at the gym and outside of it. She'd put a Herculean effort into maintaining contact with a former client who wanted nothing to do with her. Suzette hadn't ever fallen apart like this, and it served as a wake-up call.

"Well, I get how you feel, but personally, my blood is boiling! I'm fighting mad. Those bitches stole my bank card, and I wanna make 'em regret it," Angel said.

"If we let 'em slash our tires and do nothing, it's like saying you may as well slash the other two," Jake said.

"Great! So you slash their tires, and they come back at us, on and on until we get squashed because there are six of us, and who knows how many of them? Do the math, Jake!" Suzette snapped.

"Yeah, it's the math that's troubling me. We're all annoyed, humiliated, cowed, and pissed off. Which emotion do we give the most weight to at this moment? It's a tricky question, and I know who has the answer. It's some fixer guy by the name of Balcom, who's the string-puller behind all this stuff. Now we're supposed to go back to him crying and begging for help, so he can play us further? If he'll just fix everything for us, then exploit us for whatever favors he wants. It isn't him, though; someone has paid him a lot of money to hire his henchmen and con women in this badly acted charade. Should we give in to him and pay whatever god-awful price he asks? Things won't get better, and there is some invisible and unknown character free to hire another outfit to shake us down, rattle our confidence, and make us want to quit. Balcom never reveals his clients, and we have to sweep up his messes for him in exchange for his good graces. In the old days, it was called protection money," Wade said.

"So he's mob, then?" Suzette asked.

"No, he'd love it if we believed that, though. I think he is what he says: a fixer, a well-paid guy with tons of contacts on both sides of the law who can bribe, intimidate, or otherwise steer people into dropping their activities. We aren't well known; how is he digging up so much dirt on us to know where and when we bank, our names, and why the interest in a case we're working for free? It sure isn't the family working on this, so who? Who stands to gain from our packing up shop?" Wade asked.

"There is something else; the girl I grabbed with the bottle dropped her phone, and I nabbed it. There's gotta be some information we can use in there," Angel said.

"Give it to Stan," Jake said.

"So it looks like we go talk to our fixer friend," Ray said.

"We have to be very careful; this guy could just as easily send the Chief of Police after us, for all we know. We'll have to talk to him somewhere very private, and he'll never agree to that," Wade said.

"I know a place," Ray said.

"Where?" Jake asked.

"Do you know that restaurant above the Planetdome Theater? It's always jammed, right? That's only because people go there the same night as the theater events. One time Suze and I went in there when the theater was closed, and it was just the owner of the whole big restaurant. There was one old man drinking himself blind, and the owner kept going into the kitchen to cook the food himself. What's worse is that he is a chain smoker, and that restaurant is on the top floor. Suze went to complain about how long everything was taking, and she caught him sneaking up to the roof for smoke breaks. He even tilted the camera away so people wouldn't see how many smoke breaks he took. If we went in and ordered a bunch of food to keep him busy, the door to the roof would be unlocked, and we could discuss *anything* we want," Ray said with a crooked grin.

"It's true; that place is huge, and only one guy is there when the dome isn't in use," Suzette confirmed.

"Suze, so you're good with things now?" Ray asked.

"No, I am not, Ray. Don't you see what is going on here? We are becoming just like them. We are a cult! None of us ever see our families, for those of us that have any, and we use weapons and intimidation to get what we want. We manipulate and push back hard when people mess with us! What's the difference? Inch by inch, we are becoming what we hate and everything we're against. It used to be that we'd go because they couldn't intimidate us; now we go to intimidate them! What are we becoming?" Suzette challenged.

"We don't kidnap people, and we don't kill. I'd say that puts us on the right side of things," Angel said.

"I've got something else," Stan said.

"This chick's name is Rita, and we have her boyfriend's name too, but he looks like a scrawny wimp, not the type to be in on this. Also, the redhead's name is Sasha, and without her hair all twisted up and her sunglasses off, she could all but pass for Suzette. Not identical and her voice is different, but their resemblance is uncanny," Stan said.

"Which means with a bit of makeup and the right wig, I could pass for her just as easily," Suzette said.

"Sounds like you're back on board suddenly," Ray said.

"There's no time for semantics when we have work to do," Suzette said, looking more determined than ever.

Chapter 7

⊕ld Gh⊕sts and ⊕ld Ways

Deneige called just as plans were being finalized to settle scores and learn who was footing the bills against them.

"Wade, I just got off the phone with a detective from the Ridgebreak Falls Police, and it was horrible! I kept waiting for you to call, but I couldn't wait any longer. Why haven't you called?" Deneige asked frantically.

"We had a few issues to sort out over here. I'm sorry. What did he say?" Wade asked.

"It's so awful that he didn't want to give me details, but I freaked out at him and screamed into the phone, and then he told me more than I wanted to hear," she said.

"What was said?"

"They buried her alive. They duct-taped one eye shut so the other one bulged in response, and they made a small hole in the casket right above her eyes so she could see the tiny trail of earth and sand trickle into her open eye and died unable to wipe the falling dirt from going into her eye!" Deneige said, before sobbing uncontrollably.

"It can't be!" Wade said.

"What do you mean?" she asked.

"It doesn't figure. Maybe it's not her," Wade said.

"No, Ameripol pointed them to a few new details, and they've matched the DNA; it's Melanie. Why do you think it wouldn't be her?"

"I don't know. It just doesn't sound like something that a cult would do. They enjoy watching the demise of their victims. This sounds more akin to individual psychopathy or the fear tactic of a criminal organization that wants to be bigger than it is. It doesn't fit," Wade said.

"Well, it happened! I'm sorry it doesn't match your criminal profile!" Deneige said.

"Oh, I'm so sorry; I'm not thinking straight. How about I shut up and just listen until you're done?" he asked.

"It's okay. I've gotta go. I've gotta go," she said, and hung up.

He walked over to Suzette, who was studying the videotape and impersonating the mannerisms of Sasha.

"Suzette, I know you're busy, but that case up in Ridgebreak Falls isn't adding up for me. Can you see what you can find out about a ritual duct-taping one eye shut in burials? It doesn't sound right to me," he said.

"Ridgebreak Falls, again! Why are you so friggin' obsessed with this case? Is it the hottie? You can't undo murders, you know. You never wanted to go up there and look, and now you can't leave it alone. We have also been incurring a lot of expenses, while you give our work away for free," Suze said.

"You're right, but I'm going to have our losses recompensed. Can you check when you get some free time as a favor, please?" he said.

"Sure, but you do realize this case might be the very reason that the entire world is crashing down around us, right?"

"I wholeheartedly agree," Wade said.

"So who's going to pay us, then?"

"You'll see," he said.

Then he went to his room to check on Riley.

"Should I do this? Maybe I'm losing it," he said to his dog.

The German shepherd returned his gaze and barked once.

"Oh, that's a yes, my friend," he said.

He pulled Balcom's card and called him.

"Mr. Balcom, it's Wade from the bank, a few days ago," he said.

"Ah, yes, Mr. Wade at last. What can I do for you?"

"Well, I have some concerns and felt you might be of service. I don't like phones very much, so I was wondering if I could make a proposal to you in person," he said.

"Sure, you can come to my office anytime. How about Thursday?"

"Oh, I don't like offices much; too many suits and ties for me, and I'd feel like a ship out of water. How about the restaurant above the Planetdome theater? It's always busy; there are lots of people around, and if either of us sees anyone we don't like, we can ditch before we even say hello. What do you think?" Wade asked.

"Alone, just you and I, table for two?"

"That, or you can bring your 'roid monkeys, and we can have a free-for-all. I just wanted to set terms through discussion. If that doesn't suit you, then I'll know I'm in a rigged poker game anyhow," Wade said.

"No, no, you mustn't panic; we can talk, of course. When?"

"I'll be there on Thursday at 2:00 PM. If I see your goons, I split," he added.

"And what about your friends?"

"They're all scared shitless. I'm on my own here."

"2:00 PM then," Balcom said, and hung up.

The restaurant was The Top of the Planet, but everyone just called it the Planetdome, like the theater. It was very spacious and spread out wide, with lots of tables. They had green tablecloths and white napkins with thin vases and plastic flowers that were swapped out for real ones during large events.

At one table near the entrance sat Ray and Suzette. Ray and Jake were the only ones they'd never seen before and would be taken for a random customer. Suze had dyed her hair blue and had it permed, and she wore a loud, purplish shade of lipstick. Everyone was satisfied that she would not be recognized. At the far end of the restaurant sat

Jake, who'd requested to sit in a closed-off section of the restaurant, explaining to the owner that he was agoraphobic and paid an extra fifty to stay at a distance so he could not be seen from the door. Ray had ordered three salmon steaks, and Suze had ordered sushi and a garden salad. Wade ordered spaghetti and meatballs, while Jake ordered steak and lobster, guaranteeing the owner would be far too busy to check on his customers. Stan entered after the orders were placed and stayed in the washroom unseen until Ray would alert him to come out. There were no other patrons present.

Balcom entered the restaurant with his cell phone in hand and then placed it in his shirt pocket with the line open. He took no special notice of Ray and Suzette when he took a seat at Wade's table.

"It's a little quiet here, isn't it?" Balcom asked.

"Better for a private conversation, and the wine selection is astounding, by the way," Wade said.

"Well, I'm a little more interested in the issue at hand. You're having some difficulties, I'd imagine."

"Buckets full, and I'm sure you can help. What I really need is some information, but I also need to know if you'll be honest with me. What assurances can you provide?" Wade asked.

"The proof comes with the track record. I make problems disappear, and I don't make mistakes. My resume speaks for itself, and it's flawless," Balcom said.

"Okay, so who hired you to rattle us?"

"Hahaha, that'd be privileged information. How could you ever trust someone who sold out clients?"

"Exactly!" Wade said, as he saw Ray heading for the washroom.

"So what would you have me do for you?"

"What prices do you charge?"

"Oh, you just pack up your little band of troublemakers and look for another town, and I think you'll lead a pretty problem-free life. Well, as much as can be expected anyhow," Balcom said, grinning.

"I like your shoes. Of course, they wouldn't work for me because I hate laces. Maybe it's laziness, but those four little eyelets for all that lace would indicate you could trip even if you think you've tied a perfect bow. You might fall and land flat on your face if you're not careful," Wade said, staring fiercely into Balcom's eyes.

"Don't get tough with me, kid; I don't like it. Do you see this phone? I've got two of the most formidable men you'll ever see in your life, and they're listening right now. Would you like me to call them up presently?"

"Nah, that's alright," Wade grinned.

Stan, who'd been in the men's room, reached around from behind Balcom's neck, and placed him in a chokehold, pulling him from his chair. Ray followed, grabbed the man's feet, and stretched him out to carry him. Wade collected the cell phone as Stan and Ray moved down a corridor by the kitchen and made their way to the roof. Wade spoke into the phone as he followed them.

"Hey, your boy is in trouble! There is a dentist and two security guards in the basement who are going to fix his teeth permanently, and who can trust dentists? Look for him on the elevator heading down. Better hurry!" Wade said.

Suzette stood in front of the elevator by the restaurant as Big Jake called out to the owner in the kitchen.

"Your customers have all left!"

"Wha-at?" the owner said, wiping his hands on a cloth.

"The guy sitting by himself who ordered the spaghetti got an important call and said to give you this for your trouble and to apologize," Jake said, handing the man five hundred dollars.

"Of all the crazy things," the owner said.

"Well, there is nobody here, so would you mind if I smoked?" Jake asked.

"Hell, you just gave me a fiver, and to tell you the truth, I've been hankering for one all day myself," he smiled.

The two men smoked and chatted while Jake enjoyed his lobster and the owner ate one of Ray's salmon steaks. Suzette saw the light above the elevator, indicating it was almost due. She coughed twice as Jake excused himself to visit the men's room.

Two bulky men in suits rushed into the restaurant, turning their heads quickly, scanning the empty tables.

"Hey, did you see a guy in a dark gray suit in here? He was supposed to be here!" the bulkier of the two asked.

"No, I'm the owner. Nobody's here except some Native guy in the washroom. Everyone else left."

"Is there another way out of here?" he demanded angrily.

"Just the elevator; the stairwell's locked," he said.

Suzette took the next elevator down, followed the men to their cars, and photographed the license plate.

Meanwhile, there was an ugly conversation taking place on the roof after Ray had placed a piece of rebar through the door handle and lodged it in between the metal fire door frame, securing it shut until they were inclined to remove it.

Outside, the men's hair blew wildly in the crosswind as the direction of the conversation grew more chilling than the elevated breeze.

"So, you lied to me when you said you never make mistakes, isn't that right?" Wade asked with steel in his eyes and all trace of humor withdrawn from his flat, measured tone. His cadence was even, and his compassion might have been left in the glove compartment of the Jeep as a slow, quiet anger drove his pointed words.

Stan moved the fixer's head forward to simulate his nodding in agreement, while the fixer's eyes bulged with a peculiar bond of anger and fear. His face reddened, partially in disbelief that these young men had so easily tricked him, and the uncomfortable wrestling match between arrogance and crumbling pride collapsed before the unthinkable, as reality launched a mortar shell through the ballooned up walls of his ego. He clung in vain to the idea that he was still in control of a situation where the mice had just collared the cat and were about to have their way. He considered himself their superior by leaps and bounds, but his uncertainty about being released was mounting. Still, he clung to the idea they wouldn't hurt him too badly—maybe a few punches and kicks while on the ground. He could endure that, he felt. He might be able to charm them into seeing the futility of what they were doing and how they didn't want to go to jail. In the span of a few seconds, the demeanor of these helpless mice grew from long-tailed lab pawns to that of rabid sewer rats, then ultimately to feral wolverines. He was such a good talker; he could convince most people of anything. He'd have to maintain his posture as someone higher up in society than them if he were to have any chance of gaining the upper hand. Not even the potential danger he was facing was enough to suppress his brewing revenge fantasies. If he got out of this, they'd rue the day they dared to confront him.

"See, the first mistake you made was the shoes. Laces are inferior and don't really have the binding strength needed for the job. Well, not those ones, anyway. We're going to test them out to prove it to you, so you'll be sure," Wade said.

Stan forced Balcom up on the roof railing and balanced him on it. Ray intuitively tied his shoelaces to the railing.

"Do you think they can hold you up?" Wade asked.

"You sent two heavies to beat me up, and now you don't want to answer us?" Stan asked with a bemused grin. Then he pushed him backward, knocking him off balance as Balcom's weight shifted off of the ledge. Stan instantly grabbed his tie and pulled him forward after making him think he was falling. It was a display of trained hand speed that let Balcom know just how precarious a position he was in. If Balcom fell by mistake, he now knew, without a trace of doubt, that Stan wouldn't lose a moment's sleep over it.

"You sent guys to cut our tires; maybe I'll start cutting your tie then," Ray said.

Stan pushed him again with his left hand while clutching his tie with his right hand, and Balcom struggled to keep his feet on the railing. This time, the presence of real fear revealed itself on his face. His eyes were still bulging but no longer enraged, and his face was now white rather than angry red as before.

"You think stealing people's bank cards is a big joke? Oh, that was a mistake big enough to cost you all your worth right there," Wade said.

"You want money!" Balcom said, almost spitting, looking angry all over again.

"No, you owe us money! Another mistake, and you grossly underestimated us! Mistake after mistake! How do you explain that? And we're all dumb as fuck! We're in our early twenties, which means our brains aren't even fully developed yet, and I've never even seen the inside of a high school. We're all full of testosterone, piss, and vinegar. You can add a touch of perpetual resentment for the elites and establishment! In this case, that'd be you. You might even say that we aren't responsible for our own actions. You get a group of guys like us and steal from them, close off their spending, try to get them beat up, and now you think you'll talk your way out of this?"

Stan pushed him hard enough to cause him to fall over the ledge this time, and Stan pulled him up with both hands on his tie as Balcom squealed in panic.

"Good thing he's strong, eh?" Ray said with a smile.

"Then you messed with the women in the group, and you've got to know a bunch of macho lunkheads like us aren't going to be cool with that, right?"

"I just wanted you to leave town, not to hurt anyone!"

"That's not what you said at the bar with Greg and Tony," Stan said.

"The fact is, we are so dumb, immature, and bumbling that we were able to pull one over on you. What does that say about you? Idiot of the Year, maybe?" Wade asked.

"Alright, I'll do what you want," Balcom groaned.

"You haven't even heard the terms yet; you aren't very savvy at this business stuff, are you?"

"What terms, then?" Balcom shouted.

"You messed with the wrong guys, fixer, and then you went after my girlfriend! Humiliated her in public! Do you think I care about keeping my nose clean to save you? Your next sex partner is going to be the pavement ten stories down. Look at that guy right there and tell me he'll find it in his heart to spare you, ya dumbass!" Ray shouted, pointing at Stan.

The fixer sized him up while doubt and fear multiplied across his face.

"I'm gonna need your bank card to pay back Angel and get new tires," Ray said.

"You're going to need to call the bank and have them up your daily spending limit too. You've got a big wedding this weekend and are planning some very expensive gifts!" Stan said.

"It sucks when people think they can just take your money off you, but it's information I want. Now listen carefully! Who hired you to mess with us? I'm not going to ask you twice," Wade said, looking over the edge of the railing.

Balcom balked.

"He hasn't pissed himself yet; maybe he thinks we're joking," Stan said.

"Grab a shoe, Stan," Ray said.

The two men hung Balcom over the edge of the railing by his feet, giving him a clear view of bypassing traffic, as his defiance left him and he began screaming in a high-pitched voice.

"Alriiight! Alriiiight!"

Ray pulled his end up, but Stan wanted more squirming, so he faked dropping him by a foot or so before pulling him up.

"Lorne Feland hired me, but he's not the type to toy with, so I wouldn't get any big ideas, or they'll be looking for you in the foundations of construction sites," Balcom said.

"Call him right after you call the bank," Wade said.

Balcom called the bank and convinced them to increase his limit for three hours. Ray took the card and PIN number and gave them to Suzette to withdraw funds while still in her blue-haired disguise. Jake came up and replaced Ray's approach with his own energy during questioning.

"So this is the piece of puke that gutted my tires and left me stranded downtown, right?"

The only sound was the wind blowing as Balcom's eyes dropped, staring at his feet.

Jake grabbed the phone and fished through the contacts.

"Just a second; he has a call to make first. Tell him you changed your mind and are letting us go, and you're keeping his money, or you're going sidewalk swimming," Wade said.

"I can't," Balcom protested as collectively angered eyes turned upon him.

"Make it good!" Jake growled at his lowest pitch.

"Oh, alright!" Balcom said, grabbing his own phone from Wade.

"Hello, Mr. Feland, it's me, Balcom. Yes, I know. Well, circumstances have changed. This idea with those kids just doesn't seem feasible anymore. I think they have friends on the force, and I'm not taking any chances with them, and that's going to have to be final. I'm sorry. Uh, no. No, I can't do that, and I'm afraid the money's been spent already," Balcom said.

Balcom pulled the phone from his ear momentarily, and then it went dead.

"Satisfied?" Balcom groused.

"Let me see that," Jake said, grabbing his phone.

"A pro basketball player, hm. A judge, and, hey, a senator. I want the names of all the girls who stole my girlfriend's bank card. Every. Single. One. I want the names of all your clients too, and then I'm going to post all their contact information all over the web. Then I'm going to brag that I got it from you and test your popularity after that.

Well, you are the one that likes to screw around with people, right?" Jake spat the words venomously.

Balcom paled a little again as Jake looked over his fingers.

"These guys are just playing footsie with you up here; I'm a fuckin' Indigenous person, and I hate white people, so you invaders can all pay the price as far as I go, and right now I think you've got too many fingers, asshole!"

He winked at Wade and then put his fist around Balcom's pinky, testing its dexterity. Balcom snatched his hand away and started shouting.

"Look, it was just business! Money for services! I didn't know any of you guys!"

Jake called Suzette.

"Hey, little lady, there is a pervert up here with no pants on, and he's flashing all the women in the surrounding buildings. He's playing with himself and waving his pants around like a flag. Can you call the police non-emergency line from a payphone and describe him, please?" Jake said.

"What are you doing? You really want me talking to the cops? Let's negotiate," Balcom whined.

"Oh, yeah, because we have all your contacts, and we'll be letting them know about your relationship with the cops, and they don't like perverts in jail to begin with. We know people inside, and we are sure they don't like pervert snitches at all. Now give me your pants!" Jake said.

"Fuck that!" Balcom said.

Jake shoved him off balance, grabbed his belt, pants, and under-wear, and attached them to the rebar, and using his height and length, mounted it above the door to the stairwell where Balcom couldn't reach.

"I have all your contacts! One word about us to cops, and you're going to need your own fixer because we've got people on the inside, and they aren't nearly as nice as we are, asshole."

Jake dialed 911 and tossed Balcom's phone back to him. They began locking the stairwell door from the inside and left him to await the police with no pants on.

"Don't do this!" Balcom said slowly.

"Oh, you can fix it; you're a fixer who never makes mistakes!" Wade said.

"If you're a good boy we'll mail you your bank card with some balance left, if not...eh," Ray said.

"That should be alright, and we can even keep Suzette happy that we never even left a bruise on him," Jake said, grinning as widely as he ever had.

"Think he'll talk?" Wade asked.

"Not if he's smart," Jake smiled.

CHAPTER 8

A DARK PROPOSAL

The next day, Angel returned to the farmer's market, where she'd had her bank card stolen. Once again, Angel grabbed some fresh fruit and vegetables and went up to pay for them, and once again, a redhead with her hair spun in a twist under a kerchief came up to her and snatched the bank card from her hand.

"Hey, that's my bank card! What are you doing?" Angel shouted.

The redhead picked up a pop bottle, broke it against a display shelf, and waved it in front of Angel in a menacing manner.

"Somebody helllllp!" Angel cried out.

The redhead waved her middle finger at her, as an unseen voice yelled, "Sasha!"

Then she ran out of the camera frame as Ray announced he'd captured all the footage he needed and called the police. Suzette went to a nearby shopping mall, tried on some clothes at a fashion boutique, and while in the change room, removed the red wig and put a black wig on instead. She donned reading glasses, threw her shades away, and bought a new pea coat. She returned to The Pitt while Angel described Sasha to the police, indicating that she only knew her as an East End girl and that she ran with a dangerous crowd that included three other girls. Angel added that this was the second time that group had robbed her this week.

Back at The Pitt, there were looks of consternation as many unknown issues were still unresolved.

Jake handed his cell phone to Wade wordlessly. Ray moved up on the couch to hear better, Stan stopped working the heavy bag to ensure silence, and Wade put the phone on speaker mode.

"Mr. Feland, I've got a traffic ticket I'd like resolved, and I've heard you can recommend a good fixer that might get the amount reduced for me," Wade said.

"I've been expecting your call," the voice said.

"Why?"

"Well, I've come to understand some things about you, so this was the next predictable step," Feland said.

"If you can predict the future, maybe you have some stock tips for me," Wade said.

"Is that why you called?"

"No, I'd like to know why you're doing your frantic best to rattle my cage. Just exactly, what is your issue?" Wade asked.

"We should meet," Feland said.

"Agreed," Wade confirmed.

"Not in a restaurant, but there is a quiet cafe by the legislative buildings; lots of cameras; lots of security people with guns. Everyone can feel safe. I'll see you there in an hour, table for two, no more," Feland said and hung up.

"My minions and I have been awaiting your call in the wine cellar since the dark ages, and we marked the calendar for this sacred day many centuries ago," Stan said, mocking Feland's ominous tone and chuckling.

"We can't take anyone lightly these days," Jake said.

"Stan's right. This guy thinks he is the shadow of darkness. He sounds like a deranged nutjob," Ray added.

"I'll go meet Feland. You guys trickle in and get eyes on him, then describe him to Jake. He can tail him and see where he works. Keep an eye out for any thugs lurking around," Wade said before leaving.

Wade entered the cafe and examined the patio for an open seat at a small table. He saw a lean figure in a cream-colored suit, clean-shaven, with pale skin, brown hair, and a gaudy black ring on his middle finger.

"Mr. Feland?" Wade said.

"I am."

"Let's get right to it. Why are you trying to make me your worst enemy?"

"I'm not," Feland said.

"Playing games probably isn't your best move right now," Wade said, glaring at Feland.

"I think you might be in the wrong line of work," Feland said nonchalantly.

"How's that?" Wade asked.

"Well, I think you and your friends have a certain skill set uncommon to most, and I think you all feel you deserve to get paid for your troubles. This is not unheard of; there may be far more lucrative opportunities for capable people in this world than many ever even consider," Feland said dryly.

"You sound like a headhunter. You've taken steps against me and my friends, and if you think not telling me why means you get to dine undisturbed and intact, you're reading the wrong menu," Wade said, almost cheerfully.

"We've both been inconvenienced. I expect you and your compatriots have seen escalating profits over the last number of days. I've incurred costs with no returns. If this were a financial contest, you'd be declared the winner. It's inelegant to gloat," Feland said.

"There is no such thing as a one-round fight," Wade said without blinking.

"Oh, don't speak foolishly to me; you aren't stupid. You are certainly streetwise and quite astonishingly guileful. What would a man like that want with chasing phantoms around? Long-since-expired myths, ancient gossip, and secret societies, really! Seeking out the last of the Rosicrucians in case they had a glass of wine before bedding a nun? Chasing after coded notices and abandonned catacombs? Digging up the tunnels of the Freemasons? No, there's no reward in that; let's not pretend there ever could be," Feland said.

"You seem to have an interest in the past, maybe a fascination with it," Wade said.

"Your future is calling you, and I'm telling you it doesn't lurk in some relic hunter's haunted house, a feigned witches' circle, or within the contents of some dusty old tome," Feland said firmly.

"Look, I didn't come here to talk to you about the Knights Templar or anything decided in Constantinople. I want to know what your beef is, and if you don't spill, I've got three guys dying to hear you sing the high notes, and they don't care what they have to do to get you there. Tu comprends?"

"That's precisely my point. You really must learn to follow along more closely. You have some friends who are angry young men, feisty, and almost barbaric in nature, so you've all found a between-the-cracks career that allows you to harm people, often without consequence. Why not get paid for doing the heavy lifting like that with less personal risk and more reward? Ten thousand here, twelve thousand there; you could get better equipment, a better lifestyle, lawyers even, and better clothes. If you're so quick to threaten or use violence, you may even steal from those who stole from you. At your current rate, it's only a matter of time before you are all behind bars. These people you face off against, comparatively speaking, have unlimited wealth, reach, and connections. You are four men and a couple of girls against a tidal wave of corruption. Drug cartels, bikers, politicians, authorities, and the legal system itself might all be seeking your whereabouts at this very moment. How long do you think you can last against those forces? Some of these entities may be collecting resources for some of your opponents. The providers get hurt, and then the funders grow angry.

How would you fare against a multi-state bike gang? Seven corrupt cops with a shared agenda? A judge with a briefcase full of money, if he looks at you sourly? If four street toughs from parts unknown disappear, how large a scope would the search even be? However, if you could find your niche within the system, you could apply your trade far less often and experience far greater gains. You don't want to be cops; fine. You want to be muscle; fine, lots of opportunity there as well. You want to deal drugs, women, or weapons? All of those channels yield profits, and what you are engaged in comes with stunted, limited margins and the promise of a horrible death, and you know it. Do any of your group members have suicidal tendencies? Do you?"

"We didn't cut into anybody's line of business. Why are we so important to you?" Wade asked.

"I think you did, unintentionally perhaps, but that's your doing, and the only way of paying your debts over the lines you've crossed may well be to seek more noble employment. There is no balance beam to perch upon between lawful and criminal. It's one or the other, work within the system or be cast out," Feland said, glaring sternly at Wade.

"So, it's not prostitutes they want, but sex slaves they can kill after a few months, so nobody can talk about it online twenty years later. When a crew or gang owes funds for weapons, they can trade a warm body as a deal sweetener. Am I close?" Wade asked.

"How many times have you broken the rules? Ever broken your own personal code about what you would do versus what you would never do? How about your friends? Aren't they darkening their souls ever so slightly with each bad decision, and why? For vengeance, for money? How about we call them by their proper names? Wrath and greed! Why are those called deadly sins? I'd wager lust has crept into the picture somewhere along the way as well! Has it never tested your professionalism? Don't be ashamed! You are only human, and you have scores of potent agencies livid with you. Do you believe their seething will merely dissipate like a dream into the ether? You remind me of a new fish in jail who thinks he can outmaneuver an entire prison full of hardened criminals. He can't fight them all if ten or twelve have designs on him. He doesn't imagine that several hundred prisoners have bet, traded cigarettes, and had fistfights over who gets to taste the new group of fish. A dozen minnows to serve eight hundred inmates, and no friends to help them. He has to join a team to avoid being targeted as meat for the wolves, but what price to join the team, and what if the team has worse plans for him than his suitors? The pecking order has waves, those who want seconds, and those who get jealous over the fish even if when it's caught against its will. The problem is the fish didn't understand the order within the chaos.

No one cares if some rounder who calls himself a fixer gets robbed and sent to the egress. That's small potatoes, a mere indiscretion of the unwise in the dark, but tamper with the water supply of the great beasts, and they'll feast upon you without leaving table scraps. I wonder how many prisons might house a convicted cultist or three, or even ten. Going alone is never the answer. There are too many predators in the water even for a slippery little minnow. A deluded minnow imagining himself beyond reach because he dodged some Bible thumpers by smelling like yesterday's fish. Being eaten alive is standard for minnows who fail to grasp when the sharks are about to frenzy. Those that ignore the warning signs tend to get eaten first," Feland said.

"If a group of inmates ever did try to swarm me, I'd go down swinging, but I'd make sure the guy who suggested it to them got permanent injuries first. He wouldn't see it coming, and he wouldn't know who did it. I have a list in case anything ever happens to me or my pals, and you are right at the top. It'll be done with golf clubs, and they'll take their time, just so you know. You can't threaten people and offer them gifts simultaneously through the other side of your mouth. If I see you again, or ever hear your name, or if one of my friends catches a cold and his doctor gives him the wrong meds, the nine irons are coming out! So, if I were you, I'd start shopping for a nice, comfy motorized chair equipped with a piss bag," Wade said, as he got up and left his coffee untouched.

CHAPTER 9

A QUEST FOR MEANING

Back at The Pitt, Angel was smiling with pride as she brought Jake up to speed on the day's events.

"Feland looks like a problem; we threatened each other, and I made a cheap bluff about badass connections we don't have, but he wasn't bluffing. It's a standoff for now," Wade said.

"Oh, you should have seen it. Ray went to a cybercafé and emailed the cops that video of Suzette, erm, Sasha, robbing me, and they ate it up like double-stuffed donuts. I had to pick her out of a lineup, and did she ever look pissed, even when she was trying not to. It was sensational!" Angel said, beaming.

"I don't like it; you go messing with official police business like that, and you could be the one in monstrous trouble instead of her. The cops will examine that footage and study it for flaws and clues. This was reckless and dumb. There was no finesse to it; it was clumsy, and I don't like it!" Jake firmly stated to his girlfriend.

"Oh, what're you worried about? Witnesses on the scene all confirmed it was the same girl from the week before; no one knew it was Suzette. That girl is nothing less than a wizard when it comes to disguises," Angel said.

"I happen to think it was the epitome of finesse, compared with you guys who go around punching people in the head until the whole world is after us! Ugh! Gorilla want fight, gorilla hungry! Gorilla smash!" Suzette said, and pretended to pound her chest for added effect.

"I thought you were the one who said we were taking things too far, and we'll land in trouble, and now you are sending fraudulent evidence to the cops and making videos of false crime reenactments!" Jake said.

"It wasn't a false reenactment; those bitches stole my bank card! We just recreated the same scenario," Angel snapped.

"Yeah, the one where you broke a bottle and put it to someone's neck a week earlier, and you are only hoping none of the same witnesses were at the farmer's market a week later. You don't even know; it was careless, high risk, low reward, bullshit!" Jake reiterated.

"I don't see how different it was compared to what you guys did to the fixer! It's okay when the guys do it, but not the women, right, Jake?" Suzette asked.

"Don't fuckin' start that bullshit with me; it's got nothing to do with it, and you know it," Jake said.

"Okay, let's have some peace. What's the story with Feland, Jake?" Ray asked.

"Well, I don't think he works, and he's got lots of dough. He's got a real big spread on the outskirts, and a little honey that comes to see him twice a week. She is very cute, but a bit of a ditz; she has the security code for the property alarm and had to check it twice and still got it wrong. Her lips were moving, but I don't think it was voice-actuated. I think she was just unsure of herself enough to say it out loud. I was too far away to hear her, but she got it wrong twice, and I think I got the sequence on the keypad down, if we ever need to pay him a visit," Jake announced, looking insufferably pleased with himself.

"You mean, in case you ever want to break the law and perform an illegal break and enter?" Suzette asked.

"No, I mean, in case we have a good reason that goes beyond a spilled drink," Jake said.

"Like slashed tires?" Suzette asked.

"Alright, we're all the same; it doesn't matter," Ray said.

"Oh, Wade, the princess called for you; she needs to talk to you right away, and it's none of my business, but girls don't like guys they can't reach. If you don't get over your aversion to cell phones, you could lose her," Angel said.

"I'll take that under advisement," Wade said.

"Well, how are you going to take out a girl like that anyway? You don't drive because you don't have any ID. What are you going to do? Pick her up in a taxi?" Suzette asked.

"He's done it before," Stan said.

"You cannot pick up a girl like that in a taxi, Wade, no way! Even I know that!" Angel said.

"He could drive the Jeep illegally and hope he doesn't get pulled over," Stan said.

"Can anyone show me in the meeting minutes where it says my personal life should dominate all discussions?" Wade asked sarcastically.

"Aw, don't worry, Wade, we're just saving you from yourself. What about fake ID?" Suzette asked.

"He doesn't trust the quality," Jake said.

"Her parents like him, and it sounds like that doesn't happen very often. We can't let him blow it by showing up like some edgy drifter from the wrong side of the tracks!" Suzette insisted.

"But Wade *is* an edgy drifter from the wrong side of the tracks!" Ray said as everyone laughed, including Wade.

"We'll rent him a limo," Jake said.

"I'm not doing that," Wade said.

"Too late! I'm already on the phone," Suzette said.

"Someone better tell her not to order anything with mushrooms on it. We were out one time, and his date ordered something smothered in mushrooms, and he's looking at her like she's a harpy with an open wound on her forehead!" Stan said.

"Do any of you people have lives? This is not a group activity! I'm going it alone, like in Euchre, okay?" Wade asked.

"I'm making reservations for you at Casa Las Flores; you can have a top gourmet meal with great service and buy her some flowers at the same time," Suzette said.

"Who is going to pay for all this, again?" Wade asked.

"We have known a fixer, remember, and he left us a very big tip!" Jake added.

"Don't eat with your hands or throw plates!" Suzette said, giggling.

Later, at the St. James residence, Wade was welcomed in by her parents as Deniege's father poured him an overpriced Scotch, served neat.

"We've been overly protective of our daughter for obvious reasons, but we feel that you're a man of conviction and character. I want you to call me Jeremy from now on. Do you know much about Scotch, by the way?" Mr. St. James asked.

"Well, I'm not much of a drinker, but I certainly appreciate the approach of smoked cask aging; there aren't many taste experiences that continue to surprise in a multi-layered final product that others can only envy rather than rival," he said.

"One of the reasons we're so comfortable with you taking our daughter out is that we feel certain you'll bring her back to us. You will bring her back to us, won't you?" Mrs. St. James asked pointedly.

"Like my life depends on it," Wade said, not kidding in the least.

Wade understood their protective concerns, as they seemed to be evaluating him for any sign of weakness in character. At the restaurant, Wade was not the only one making an effort to avoid staring at Deneige. It felt as though all eyes were repeatedly sneaking glances at her, and even the wait staff treated her as royalty, and her full-length black dress with a long slit drew everyone's attention.

"I didn't see any cream of mushroom soup on the menu," she said.

Wade's jaw tilted slightly, and he constrained every muscle in his body so as not to betray any sign of disgust.

"I'm just kidding; I hate mushrooms," Deneige said with a guilty grin.

"Remind me to tell Ray to find a new girlfriend when I get back," Wade said, smiling.

"Your friends really love you, you know that?"

"They're just using me for my MP3 collection," Wade said.

"Oh no, Suzette told me what I should and shouldn't order, and Angel said if I break your heart, there will be no place on Earth I can hide. That's a lot of pressure on a girl who doesn't date much; I barely know the rules," she said.

"Do you see all these guys at the other tables? They are wishing you'd give them the chance to have their hearts broken, lining up in their imaginations, and the only reason they aren't asking you out right this second is because their dates are watching. You made them all forget that fact for a moment when you walked in. So, you may not be a seasoned veteran of the dating game, but forget the rules. The best girl in the room gets the spoils and can steer the game in any direction she likes. She can be the tourist along for the ride or host the feast of a lifetime. Like some Valhallan queen rewarding a fallen warrior, there is no pressure on her because she has no obligations. We are two sovereign individuals free to make any choices we like, and the only item on the agenda is simply enjoyment—the enjoyment of time spent with good food and better company. So, instead of the job interview aspect, I am going to ask you one question only: Tell me about something you cared about. It can be anything, but something you cared about far more than most people would ever expect," Wade said.

"After my sister went missing, I buried myself in dance recitals and had an imaginary friend. My folks were guarded about my going out with people, even girlfriends, so I had lots of alone time. I invented a talking monkey that kind of looked like one of my stuffed animals. Pretty weird, huh?" she asked.

"It's been said by a lot of experts that kids who are too intelligent for their peer groups often create imaginary friends. I'd wager that means you have a lot in common with the smartest people in the world," Wade said.

"And you?"

"I care about injustice, not in the social justice warrior manner, but more in the true physical abuses that go unpunished in the world, and Stan is my imaginary friend because when people look at him, they can't believe he's a real person," Wade said, chuckling.

"Well, he's not my type, but he is good-looking in a rugged sort of way, but yeah, a little scary-looking too. So, you do this kind of work to correct all the world's injustices?"

"Well, you can't right every wrong, but I just love seeing the people who get away with it all the time getting stopped in their tracks, and the shock and cognitive dissonance they go through when it's at the hands of someone they grossly underestimated. That satisfaction feeds my soul quite a bit, but I have to admit it's like trying to cross the ocean in a canoe sometimes and probably doesn't stack up as a sustainable career," Wade said.

"And your family?"

"My friends are my family; that's why they act like imbeciles over this date with you; they need to start watching soap operas instead," he grinned.

"You're like a collection of orphans acting as a surrogate family for each other, then?"

"No, we're more like wandering strays that bonded together."

"Pretty honest," Deneige said.

"Your family?" Wade asked.

"My parents both have their careers, yet they serve their roles adequately enough that I shouldn't complain. My sister was often seen as the worst kid around for miles. People felt she'd spent her time doing nothing but pulling the wings off of insects until she could do it to human beings, and while part of the story was certainly true, she had another side that people often didn't see. They think she had no compassion, but that was untrue; in fact, I'd say it was her greatest weakness," Deneige said.

"Is compassion a weakness? Really!" Wade said.

"Of course, if you think about it, she had compassion for cultists, criminals, and sadists. Any quality can be a weakness if it's pointed in the wrong direction or used improperly, no?"

"I just hadn't looked at it in quite that light, but you have a point," Wade said.

"I am passionate about a lot of things: art, music, business, longevity, and achieving goals. I have a lot of passion; I think that's my biggest failing. Being too passionate about things and having an appetite for success makes me more of a solo artist than a team player. In relationships, I always think there is a 51 percent stakeholder and someone who just wants it more. Do you think you could handle 49 percent? Do you think you'd risk giving up a little independence for a truly exhilarating experience? Do people even ask themselves such questions before they march ahead? I do, Wade, I do," she said.

"I shoot for fifty-fifty down the middle; realistic or not, I hope for an equal share at the board meeting and on the dance card. It's give and take; I can share things, but I know some women want a little more because they think about kids and the future and need some further assurances. I have no problem with that," he said.

"Oh, I care about kids a great deal. That is such a permanent step, and so many factors have to be weighed for proper rearing. One has to ensure they enjoy their lives, including their chores and duties, so they'll become functional and useful without becoming unruly as they grow. My maternal instincts are very potent; when I see an improperly raised child that's lonely or not cared for, I just wish I could adopt them and give them all my love. It's so unrealistic, but I'm a bit sappy that way. I want to have the most rewarding children ever—young people that can carry on a legacy and continue fulfilling a family tradition long after we've gone. What about you, Wade? I can't get a good read on you. You don't seem particularly enamored with money; you have no family to speak of, no spiritual beliefs per se, and a highly irregular occupation. If you disappeared tomorrow, I'd have trouble proving you were ever even here. Do you think you could be a good father? What matters most to you?" Deneige asked.

"Money matters, but it's not worth losing your soul over; people are what matter most to me. I don't

like seeing them taken advantage of for any reason. I think, as a society, we could do a lot better and quit putting our heads in the sand when we see wrongdoing because of inconvenience or the fear of being sued. There's no integrity in that. As for kids, I think you have to be honest with them and try to guide them away from too much booze and drugs so they don't throw their lives away. The ones who can handle it refute that, but the odds support it," Wade replied.

"A sermon from an atheist?" Deneige asked, grinning with a raised eyebrow.

"I'm not anti-God by any means; I'm not even anti-religion. I think there is a place for it; it provides a sense of community for lonely people, it keeps some borderline criminals in check, it celebrates family over depopulation, and it reminds people about being charitable and forgiving. It'd be pretty sad to be against all of that. What do you think?" Wade said.

"I'd caution against supporting any religious views too strongly; I doubt nearly everything at times," she said.

"I thought I might be getting into hot water there."

"Oh, no. But what of the zealots who beat their kids if they say their prayers one minute late, the sexual offenses of priests, the Jonestown and Waco massacres, the crooked popes, and the fact that the Vatican has more money than most nations? It's more like serving Mammon than God, if you ask me," she said.

"Any philosophical doctrine can be gamed by manipulators with charisma and a good memory. I'm not sure we can say they all worship demonic-level greed. You can't paint them all with the same brush, any more than you can say all atheists believe the same things. Some insist there is no god, some feel they haven't seen enough genuine proof, and others study all religions and haven't been swayed by a particular one," he said.

"So, what do you say to the zealots who say you have no soul and are like an animal living out a godless, soulless life?"

"I tell them their religion was decided by geography and not spirituality. If you grow up in a Christian country, Christ is your God. If you grow up in a Buddhist country, then it's Buddha, and so on. It gets passed down from parents to children for generations. Ancient peoples conformed to each other's beliefs regionally to avoid being cast out or burned at the stake, not because they were invited to a better life. That said, I like most religious people," he said.

"Then you have no fears of being wrong, getting up there on Judgment Day, and having to explain yourself? I know everyone thinks I'm this perfectly behaved wonder compared to my sister, but I say there are no saints down here. No one is always pure in thought and deed. I know if it were me, I'd be more worried about the collective frowns than accepting smiles in that situation, but I don't see it happening, at least not for me. People can believe anything they like," she said.

"You're honest too," Wade said, as they both smiled.

"What about your childhood?"

"I spent a lot of time outdoors until I discovered books, and then I found so many schools of thought and philosophical challenges to delve into. I nearly obsessed over all the infinite paths and entire worlds I could get lost in. And you?" he asked.

"I grew up in my sister's shadow. She got in all the fights, did all the stealing, and pulled all the school fire alarms. I think teachers were just happy that I didn't assault them. I got stuck with a 'Goody Two Shoes' label that people just couldn't let go of. Of course, labels never tell the full story, and deep down, I had all the same temptations and frustrations as any other kid. I just knew that there was no point in acting out because, for most, all that it leads to is either punishment, a bad reputation, or both. I have failings and shortcomings, and I make no pretense about them. I'm not a goddess or a movie star. I'm just another flawed individual hoping for someone who can accept my failings, my needs and wants, and really understand them," she said.

"I think I want the job as your professional understander," Wade said.

"Is it urgent?" Deneige asked coyly.

"Urgent enough."

"The word came to English in the 1590s, stemming from French, meaning pressing or impelling, but it's originally Latin. Urgentum, Urgere; to press hard, Urge!" Deneige said, grinning mischieviously.

"And the word 'abstain 'is also French, from Abstiner: to hold one-self back, and the question is; How on Earth did the word abstain arrive in the 1300s before urges did?" He said, returning her smile.

Wade paid the check, and they wandered to the veranda that over-looked another patio with multi-colored lanterns. They shared a long kiss under a starless sky, and for one moment, Wade forgot all about cults and enemies and where he fit into society. He was never so happy to be forgetful in all his life.

Later, he brought Deneige to her door, but this time he wasn't ner-vous about facing her parents, as he knew he was someone in her life, regardless of anyone else's opinion.

"You have to find yourself, you know," Deneige said.

"What do you mean?"

"You have to sate your soul with more nourishment than settling scores with cults and putting yourself at risk ad nauseam. You said as much yourself. You need to find what makes you happy, not temporarily relieved. That's like a drug addict getting his fix; it's a little less satisfying each time, and the expense keeps growing. That's no way to live your life. You need to find something more worthwhile to care about, and I'm going to help you find it," she said, looking excited and eager.

Her exuberance won him over, so he smiled. She kissed him again before entering her home, but Wade left feeling something less than wholly accepted, and he wondered if this would be any different than

Suzette's friend Monica being too polite to explain the gulf between their respective social circles.

When he arrived back at The Pitt, Angel and Suzette were watching a black-and-white movie together, and both walked up to him, taking turns asking him questions.

"Well?"

"What happened?"

"Did you kiss her?"

"Are you going to see her again?"

"What did she wear?"

Wade waved his hand in the air dismissively and kept walking toward his room.

"Are you kidding me? Tell us what happened," Suzette urged.

"Now listen, you two soul-sucking little gossip vampires! Go haunt a house! If there's anything you need to know, it'll all be in my memoirs when I'm sixty-five, and you can read about it then. Thank you for all your interest and support, but it's well past my bedtime. Good night!" Wade said.

"Fuck that noise! Did you kiss her?" Suzette demanded.

Wade turned away, suppressing a mild grin.

"He kissed her alright, and then some," Angel said.

The next day, Deneige called, indicating that the family would be holding a burial for Melanie and they would like him to attend.

"Of course, I'll come; just say what time," Wade said.

"It's at five PM," Deneige said.

"Sorry, I don't want to be indelicate, but is this the body that the police said came from a tainted grave, the one with the hole in it and all that? I only ask because I don't feel like that's really her. I think it's a mistaken identity. Did you see the coroner's report or anything? There could have been a mix-up. Sometimes the authorities feel so bad for grieving families that they might want to alleviate their grief. They could swap something just to make you feel better or to ease your pain, and I don't think it's right unless you are sure. I think your family has been through enough as it is. If there's a mistake, that could mean an exhumation, and I just want to be sure, that's all," Wade said.

"Wade, what the hell are you talking about? The DNA matched, and the police were very thorough and considerate. My parents and I are extremely grateful for all the effort you've put in, but what you are saying is outlandish. If I were to say anything about this to my parents, I think they'd find it extremely inappropriate, don't you? What's come over you? You are acting extremely strange! I can't believe this! I was just asking you to attend. If you don't want to come, just say so. You don't have to go through all this nonsense!" Deneige said.

"I'm sorry. I'll shut up about it, and I'm sorry if I sound like a lunatic. I would just feel so much better about things if I could see the coroner's report, the death certificate. If I could just see that, I'll admit I'm wrong and never mention it again. I'm sorry," Wade said.

"I'm going to hang up now. If you want to come, then come, but not if you are going to carry on like this with my parents. Goodbye," she said just before the line went dead.

Everyone but Stan stared at Wade in disbelief.

"You can all close your mouths now," Wade said.

"Sure, Wade, but can I ask what the play is here? I'm confused as hell," Ray said.

"I just want to be sure of things. Ever since we got mixed up with this case, everybody and their brother has tried to stop us. Now, after years of sitting in a dusty cold case file, the cops find a missing body in five minutes flat, and now there's just one more reason for us to drop this thing like a hot rock," Wade said.

"Okay, well, can I ask why we even are on this case that doesn't actually seem to exist? We never charged anyone any fees for it. Every slippery character from hell and their brothers want us dead, humiliated, out of business, or all of the above. Who exactly are we doing this for?" Suzette asked.

"You just found a one-in-a-million girl, and even that is getting put to the test. There are some bad people connected to this thing, powerful people with connections well beyond our grasp, and usually we don't even know who they are. If someone slipped a false report somewhere that closes the case, then maybe they did us a favor? Suppose it's not her, but the family gets closure, and we don't get hunted down by the entire crime world, and everything goes back to normal. What's the harm? Who suffers? I don't get it," Ray said.

"You're right, each of you; I've been behaving poorly. I've put everyone at risk. I should have looked into this on my own. I'll be back," Wade said before opening the door and leaving.

"What's going on with him?" Angel asked.

"Why is he so bloody obsessed with the dead sister?" Ray asked.

Thirty minutes later, Suzette came down to the TV room with an announcement.

"I just got off the phone with the coroner's office; I posed as Deneige and tried to get them to mail me a copy of the report to a P.O. box, but they wouldn't, and they also refused to email it. But I did convince him to read it to me, so we can't be sure it was the real document, but it sounded legit to me," she said.

"Let's hear it," Jake said.

"Sexual assault, blunt force trauma to the skull, both ankles broken, the cause of death was suffocation," she said.

"I'll go pick him up and tell him," Jake said.

A few minutes later, Jake pulled up alongside Wade, who appeared disillusioned.

"I might have good news for you; I'm not sure. Suze talked to the coroner's office; they said sexual interference, two broken ankles, trauma to the head, and suffocation. Does that help clear things up?" Jake asked.

"Yes, it confirms the body they are giving to the St. James's is *not* Melanie's," Wade said.

CHAPTER 10

WISDOM VERSUS MORALITY

Wade helped himself to one of the cold cut sandwiches, which were cut into triangles and skewered with toothpicks to hold them together. They were set on a plate among other assorted dishes that the family had laid out for guests in the dining room. Mrs. St. James encouraged him to have more, but he didn't feel like eating. His feelings of opposition to this funeral were bubbling to the surface, but he knew if he said a word on the subject, it wouldn't go over at all. Wade watched as a few relatives were introduced, and he all but shied away from conversing with them, as the idea of playacting and bowing his head as the casket of some unfortunate "Jane Doe" was lowered into the ground while her family ached for closure was weighing heavily on him. Each member of the cult-tracking group had cautioned him earlier today about wielding his honesty like a medieval mace in search of its next victim. It was his first time in a three-piece suit, and he felt surprisingly at ease in it. This was not enough to settle his stomach, however, as the urge to leave for fear of speaking out against a false funeral versus staying and stifling his overwhelming suspicions seemed equally unbearable.

"Not hungry?" Mrs. St. James asked.

"Well, one more shouldn't slow me down too much," he said as he drew a second snack.

"Wade's something of a carnivore; he lives mostly on eggs and meat," Deneige said.

"Oh, well, perhaps he can stay over in the guest room, and we'll make him an omelet in the morning," Mrs. St. James said.

"Let's not chain the man to the house, dear; he may have outside obligations. Of course, you are welcome, Wade, but only if you have room in your schedule," Mr. St. James said.

"Well, I only have one outstanding obligation, and I want to assure you how honored I am that you would even consider me as your houseguest, so thank you both very kindly. But if I could be excused for a brief while, I could take care of my business and free up the rest of the evening. Would that be alright?" Wade asked.

"Certainly, Wade, you take care of your endeavors, but may I ask what's so pressing?" Mrs. St. James inquired.

"Of course, it's to do with you and this entire situation. You see, I'm something of a detail freak—or a stickler for correct details, at least—so whenever I get a sense that a crucial one is missing, obfuscated, misarranged, or glossed over, it troubles me a little. I don't have obsessive-compulsive disorder, but the more important the situation, the more troubling I find missing details to be," Wade confessed.

"Alright, but you said it has to do with us. How?" Mr. St. James said.

"Well, there was something I wanted to look into that, if it's a non-issue, probably wouldn't be worth mentioning, but if by some chance an incongruency proved problematic, I'd feel an obligation to share it with you," Wade said.

"Now, you've got us all intrigued, Wade; what's on your mind?" Mr. St. James said.

"Oh, no," Deneige said in an exasperated tone.

"I'm very sorry to bring this up after all you've been through; in fact, I'd rather avoid this subject altogether, but I have some qualms about the information you've been given," Wade said sheepishly.

"You cannot be doing this right now!" Deneige said.

"Doing what?" Mrs. St. James demanded.

"I'm concerned the remains being provided to you are not correct," Wade said quietly.

"You what?" Mr. St. James asked.

"You just had to, right, Wade?" Deneige chided.

"And just how exactly would you have knowledge of, or hold insight as to whether, those remains are correct unless you know something you aren't telling us? What kind of inside information is being kept from us? Were you present when she died? Did you have something to do with her death? Did you kill our daughter and take her from us?" Mrs. St. James said this with her voice cracking and tears building up in her eyes.

"Are you some sick son of a bitch? All the free services, all the interest, and now you are after our other daughter! Are you a complete, raging psycho?" Mr. St. James hollered.

"No, I'll offer you my wrist and tell you I had nothing to do with your daughter's death; if you see one trace of a lie, you can cut me," Wade said.

He drew a large kitchen knife from its rack, placed the handle in Mr. St. James's hand, and rolled up his sleeve. He then turned his wrist upward, exposing soft veins before Mr. St. James's knife hand.

"I've never harmed a hair on the head of either one of your daughters and never would. I only want justice—or the closest we can come to it—for Melanie and your family! Cut me if I'm lying. Cut me!" Wade roared at the father of his new girlfriend.

"Well, maybe not, but you have to admit you've got a pretty peculiar involvement here. I still want to know how you can be so certain that DNA-verified remains, confirmed by the police, that you've never seen aren't legitimate. How do you explain that?" he asked, putting the knife back on its rack.

"People have been trying to get me to turn my attention away from this subject since I started looking into it. I find it convenient that suddenly, after years of vague platitudes and empty answers, all aspects of the matter are closed, final, and wiped away forever. I pity the next person to even ask the most harmless of questions about this, who will undoubtedly be told one of those pathetic 'moving forward' type of speeches through smug, condescending grins, rife with canary feather smiles," Wade said.

"Why are you so filled with suspicion, Wade?" Deneige asked.

"There is a missing component to the story here. Twenty percent plus seventeen percent plus five percent never equals a hundred percent. There is a why, a who, and a who'd want this topic shut down in record time question. Someone is pulling a lot of strings to make that happen, and I feel that remaining in the dark about those things might be even more dangerous than if we knew and just got on with our lives," Wade said.

"Well, you can't right every wrong, Wade," Mrs. St. James said.

"No, but there are people responsible for this and other similar actions, and I wouldn't mind seeing them punished for their troubles," he said.

"To what end, Wade?" Deneige asked.

"Until those orchestrating these things are stopped," he said.

"Then what?"

"Settle down, get a home, master the stock market, get married, have two-point-two kids, a beautiful wife, a sensible car, and a white picket fence," he said.

"I wonder," Deneige said.

The next day, Wade awoke at The Pitt to find all the couples were out, and only Stan was home practicing his martial arts techniques.

"Wanna go a few rounds, Wade?" Stan asked.

"Naw, you're too big 'n' creepy. Whenever you walk past a garden, the plants all die. Actually, I'm going away for a few days with Deneige. I've got some ground to make up for, but before I do, I need to see about something out of town first. If I don't come back by Monday noon, I want you to go and see that Feland guy. I told him we knew some heavies with golf clubs looking to improve their aim. He wears a black ring with some satanic insignia on it; that might be a membership ring to a club or order of some kind," Wade said.

"What do you want to happen?" Stan asked.

"Two things: I want Deneige protected at all costs, and if I don't come back, I'm either dead or being tortured. Try to find out whether Feland will have security or thugs, so you might have to go as a delivery guy or something. Find out whose show he's running and how many others are wearing those stupid rings. If you haven't heard from me by Friday, assume the worst and don't pull *any* punches, okay?"

Stan had been grinning over the dead plant comment, but he grew stone-faced and simply nodded chin to chest, closed his eyes, and opened them again. Wade knew he didn't have to say another word.

The St. James family held Melanie's funeral without inviting Wade, and even his closest friends felt he had been obsessing over the case without any clear goals and put everyone in danger. Overdue for a break and desperate for some alone time, he announced to the group that he'd be taking a mini holiday. He'd grown up alone and wanted to sleep under the stars in the woods without anyone questioning him or critiquing his ideas and motives. Angel gave him some herbs in a pouch—some for a health boost, some in case of a poisonous bite, and some to make his dreams more vivid in case he decided to visit the spirit world. Wade had no spiritual beliefs, didn't believe in drug use for any reason, and was inclined to say no. Angel was brutally honest about everything, often too honest, yet her loyalty to the entire group was unshakable, so he accepted the herbs and thanked her for her understanding. He kept the herbs separated to avoid confusing them, occasionally munching on the immune system boosters and leaving the rest untouched in his knapsack, perhaps for Stan.

Wade walked most of the night, expecting to tire, but the woods beckoned as he wrestled with his thoughts and motives, wondering why the lack of clarity and resolution had been wreaking such havoc with his mind. In one unsettling moment, Wade noticed the spent casing of a bullet lying flat on the earth between a weed and a flower. One found could easily indicate there might be more undiscovered. He changed directions at random; as he'd often done as a kid, there is no getting lost when the whole planet is viewed as one's unexplored backyard. People rarely discovered him when he was lost, and he missed that freedom. The stars never judged him, and the treetops that shifted in the breeze never turned their backs on him. The night sky had provided a velvet, charcoal backdrop against a multitude of glowing, tiny beacons of hope. Gradually, the Earth's night cloak softened in tone, meandering between indigo, cobalt, and cerulean blue before settling on twilight. Wade then dropped his walking stick, fell to his knees, and slumped to the ground. His eyes fell shut quickly as his body forced him to rest precisely at that moment.

The sky grew dark again, the stars seemed to fade, and in the distance, Wade heard the sound of footsteps. His eyes widened as he forced himself to sit upright despite his body feeling sluggish. He took out his knife, hollowed out the end of his walking stick, and found an errant tree root barely covered by the ground. He tugged aggressively at the root, pleased with its wiry strength and texture. Wade placed his knife into the hollowed-out portion of his improvised staff and secured it by winding the root around the stick and binding it to the knife tightly enough that it wouldn't budge. Gathering some wide green leaves beside him, he placed his newly found spear under the leaves as the footsteps grew closer. He feigned sleep, timing the sound of the footsteps crunching softly among the brush, leaves, and dead branches. They weren't heavy boots, by the sound of them, but possibly runners on the feet of this approaching stranger.

The drowsiness he felt was potent. Had it not been for his adrenaline spiking, he surely would have drifted off again. He saw movement for a second, then a quickly moving shadow. It had a certain grace, almost an elegance, like that of a cheetah or panther. As it moved closer, the ground was covered more with moss and earth than dead branches, and Wade could no longer hear its steps. He sat up and clutched his handcrafted spear under the leaves. *Time it, steady, time it precisely,* he thought, as he coiled his body tight and prepared to burst forth in one deadly strike. He quieted his breathing and put all his focus on his hearing because he couldn't pinpoint whether this shadowy body was between the trees or on the darkened ground.

"What are you doing, Wade?" he heard a female voice ask from the dark, followed by a derisive laugh.

"Not brave enough for a face-to-face conversation?" Wade asked.

"I thought I'd tormented your poor little preteen body enough last time, and I wouldn't want to interfere with your more realistic ambitions," she said.

He didn't answer, trying to locate the voice. The figure crawled up to him in a plush, purple hooded dress with an open neck and flung the hood back, revealing her face.

It was Melanie—older, more mature, and just as alluring as ever—but her expression was weathered, and there was a trace of defeat in her eyes, though her supreme confidence never wavered in his presence.

"So, you've been alive all this time? You never tried to get in touch with me at all?" Wade asked.

Melanie turned sideways and thought carefully before answering, which was out of character.

"Were you hoping we'd fall into each other's arms and run away together?"

"No, I've outgrown that delusion," Wade said.

"There's something I need you to do for me," she said.

"The royal queen of self-reliance seeks a favor?"

"I saved you from a lot of heat when you were young; I saved your life. You owe me!"

"What do you need?"

"There's a slab of stone with my name on it, and someone else's kid is rockin' my box, if you catch my drift. Do you like people sleeping in your bed when you're not home?" Melanie asked.

"So, tell your folks; they'll flip when they see you. They care about you!" Wade said, grinning widely.

"No can do, wide-eyes. You have to do it."

"Why?" Wade asked, narrowing his gaze.

"You want my prissy little kid sister, right?"

"Yes, and don't call her th—"

"She could love you or hate you just as easily. Often, the most terrifying thing about human beings is what they believe in." She added with abrupt laughter.

"That sounds more like you, actually," Wade said.

Melanie walked closer to him and embraced him. She pressed her chest into his, raised her neck, and moved her lips toward his. He pulled back and turned away from her.

"You owe me, Wade!" Melanie said scornfully.

She drew closer again, and as he looked into her eyes, he couldn't believe their family resemblance, but he was overtired, and in his state, Melanie was beginning to look more like Deneige. Wade knew that if a trick of the light could fool a person, certainly a trick of the dark could play with the perceptions of an overtired hiker.

"You *owe* her, Wade!" Deneige said as she disrobed, allowing the hooded dress to fall around her.

She walked to a rocky lake edge and stood over the water. The moon seemed to grow in the distance, creating a sexy silhouette of her every contour.

"If she can't rest, neither can I!" Deneige said, scornfully.

She turned and raised one knee, placed her foot along her standing knee like an art statue, and dove into the water. The shimmering water lost its moonglow reflection as the water turned black, yet no one surfaced. Wade looked up, and there was no moon in the sky; the stars were gone, and the forest offered no glimpse of even fractured light as all went dark.

Wade opened his eyes to a sky of Prussian blue and the sounds of birds chirping and chipmunks chasing each other around in the trees. He'd been out for hours, and his dream had been far more vivid than any before. He examined his knapsack to discover that the herbs had bounced around, and he undoubtedly took the wrong batch. He'd consumed hallucinogenic herbs, possibly psychotropic ones, and he didn't even know how long he'd been under the effect, how long he'd been asleep, or even what day it was. He had no bearings other than the sun's position, and was utterly lost. Normally, he relied on his bushman's skills, but he wasn't entirely sure if what he was seeing was actually real.

He evaluated his priorities: food, safety, shelter, and direction. Then he remembered his conversation with Stan.

If I'm not back by Friday, assume the worst and don't pull any punches. What if it were Friday? He felt his cheek for beard growth and decided he'd been out for a couple of days. His watch was left behind as time was the last thing he wished to dwell on. He found water and followed it downstream. His misspent youth taught him that if one followed water upstream, it could lead to a narrow spring somewhere with no one around, but if one followed downstream, they would almost always find people. He walked at a quick pace rather than exhausting himself by running. Wade found an abandoned campsite, and while unoccupied, it had a dirt road that connected it to other roads. Wade ditched his walking stick to appear more favorable to those who might pick up a hitchhiker.

After an hour, he saw a compact Jeep and waved his arms out in front of himself, smiling. The Jeep slowed down, and the driver lowered his head to peer out the window and gave a cautious stare at Wade before hitting the accelerator, driving off ahead of a dissipating cloud of dust.

Two more hours passed before another vehicle approached; it was a red Ford Bronco with lit-up brake lights that stopped about twenty-five paces ahead of Wade.

He ran up to the waiting vehicle and eagerly grabbed the door handle, but it was locked. The passenger window lowered about one inch as the driver peered through it, sizing up Wade before asking a few questions.

"Hey there, what are ya doin' out here?" the driver asked.

"I was out hiking and lost my way. I'm looking to head back to civilization or even the nearest phone," Wade said, smiling.

"So yas just came all the ways out here, and now you're lookin' for a phone?"

Wade peered into the window to see a fairly large man, a few pounds overweight, with an untrimmed goatee, sporting a ball cap and sunglasses, who was acutely aware that he held all of the power in this conversation.

"I just came to be close to nature for a while and eventually lost my way. It sure was nice of you to stop," Wade said.

"Nice enough for sure; I'm just a bit concerned about who I let into my truck, y'understand?"

"Can't be too careful these days," Wade said.

"Ya look like ya been around some," the driver said.

"Up the river and down the stream," Wade said with a chuckle, uncertain of what was being asked of him.

"Well, where'd ya go to school?"

"School?" Wade asked in a surprised tone.

The truck accelerated and drove about ten paces further up the road. Wade contemplated some rude commentary but knew he had to be amenable if he were to spare Stan from a very risky situation. This wasn't about tolerating an obnoxious travel companion; it was about saving Stan from an unnecessary dance with untold danger. He trotted up to the passenger window and tried again.

"Didja remember where ya went to school yet?" the driver asked.

"Mountain Hills Elementary, and dropped out before high school," Wade said.

"Never heard of it, and that's a pretty dumb name for a school," the man at the wheel said.

"It's out of state, and I can't help the name," Wade said with a shrug, still smiling.

"You don't sound like ya never went to high school!" the man said.

"I was a bit of a bookworm. Every day that passes, I think I should've stayed in school," Wade added.

"Ever robbed anybody?"

"You mean like robbing someone of their dignity because they are in a tough spot? No!" Wade said.

"Well, I was about to turn around and head back to my brother-in-law's place, but he ain't got a phone, and there's nothing much along the way. If I was to take you to a phone, there's a bar out in Skittsville, but that's goin' far outta my way," he said.

"Well, I could always throw in for the gas," Wade said.

He spoke in slow, evenly measured words so that no trace of his temper might be detected. At this point, he would be happy to overpay just to make his phone call, but his distaste for predatory opportunists was rising, and he had to stifle it.

"Well, how much ya got on ya?" the driver asked.

"I could throw in twenty-five for the trouble," Wade said.

Once again, the truck accelerated about ten paces ahead. Wade walked up to the vehicle this time.

"Okay, I get it now. I'll give you three hundred dollars to take me to the nearest payphone, and I'll throw in the twenty-five as a tip when we get there, but there's a catch. If you try to gouge me again, the deal is off. If you run out of gas, overheat the engine, pop a piston, or get a flat, the deal is null and void. Agreed?"

The man reached out his hand to take the money, but Wade pulled it away, displaying unusually quick reflexes.

"You'll have to unlock the door first," Wade said coolly.

Wade walked around to the passenger side and waited for the door lock to sound.

"Ya gotta give me the money before we get goin'," the man said.

"Of course, unlock the door."

The two men drove with some forced small talk that flittered away shortly after it started each time, so the sound of the engine and bouncing suspension served as a syncopated rhythm section in search of a melody. The silent tension between passenger and driver hung in the air like a rancid fog of insecticide clouding over two germophobes.

After about ten minutes, the engine began to overheat. Smoke escaped from under the hood and rushed along the truck until the windshield offered scant visibility, and the driver pulled over.

"She's overheated! There ain't jack I can do about that," he said.

"Uh, you should open the hood; I'm mechanically inclined," Wade said.

"Well, maybe y'are, n' maybe y'aren't. I gotta be careful who I let work on my truck," the driver said.

"You mean you'd rather be stranded than let me take a look?" Wade asked.

The driver went and popped open the hood, watching Wade with his arms folded. Wade examined the engine, then crawled under the car for one second and immediately pulled himself up. Earlier, when he'd ditched his walking stick, he retrieved his knife and placed it in his sock so as not to alarm any potential rides.

"Now, you remember how I said if anything like this happened, our little deal was null and void? Well, I've got a feeling you don't want to give me my money back now, do you?" Wade asked.

"Well, I've got repairs to make because of you. If I hadn't picked you up, my truck would be just fine!" he said.

"I had a feeling you were going to say that," Wade said, smiling.

Wade crawled under the truck and took out his knife, carving a huge slice through the exhaust manifold and jamming the blade into the radiator hose, then replaced the pocketknife into his sock.

"Now what 'n' hell dja you do, just there?" The driver asked watching the fluid drip down.

"Yeah, we sure are stranded alright. Who could have known such a thing might happen?" Wade asked, in an exaggeratedly naive tone.

"Damn it! I shoulda never picked you up. Now the truck is scrapped, and we both gotta figure out a way home," the driver shouted.

"Well, I think we can manage. To save you some of that performance art, let me tell you my plan! First, you should tell me that just beyond the next hill, or close to it, there is a fork in the road, and that our best chances are to split up to get help. I'll be convinced to take the dead end, and you'll take the one that has a hidden vehicle about a quarter of a mile up the road. It also has a three-gallon bladder full of coolant to make up for all that dripped through the loosened drainage cap under the rad—no need for repairs—and you can repeat the same trick next week. Now, normally, if we were in the city, there would be a couple of guys waiting in the next car, but you hate that idea because you are a greedy control freak. You perfected the con so no one can rat you out, and you don't have to cut anyone in on the take. You've got two sets of keys: one clipped to your pants pocket and the other clipped to your belt. You keep them on a clip because you can't risk losing a set—it's a dead giveaway that you're a control freak. You didn't bring a gun because if you were caught, the sentence would be too brutal for someone like you. I know the signs, trust me! We can fistfight for the keys, and I could spend an hour looking for the second vehicle, or you can keep the three hundred and drive me to the nearest phone—a phone that'll be way closer than Skittsville—and you get to keep all your little scams and your teeth. I'll never mention anything to the cops because I've got more pressing matters than you to deal with.

Your call," Wade said.

"You think you're pretty tough, doncha?" the driver said.

"It's not that; it's just that I've got commitments that I can't dodge, and I'm far more committed to reaching my goals than you are. Now, I'm pretty sure you've got a knife or a taser or something nearby to tilt the odds in your favor, but you aren't reading the situation correctly. If I can't meet my obligations because I wasted so much time with the likes of you, things aren't going to stop when one person drops out cold. If you get the upper hand, you have to figure out what to do with me, but if I get the chance to even the score with you after I break a number of bones and cave in your face, I'm going to find that car and drive you to a stairwell. Then I'm going to lay you down on those stairs and jump up and down on your legs until I hear them snap like popsicle sticks, and I am going to leave you there, broken-limbed, crawling around, and crying for mercy. Now that the stakes are on the table, are you in or out, fuckhead?" Wade asked, glaring.

"Bite me," the man said and instantly spat in Wade's eyes.

This afforded him a moment to draw a bone-handled knife from his pocket.

Wade quickly wiped the spit from just below his left eye, regaining his combat stance with fists up. He kicked the man just above his left knee, forcing it to bend in reverse of the way it normally would with a snap kick, and rushed a punch to the man's mouth, splitting his lip, while he was already falling down.

He got up swinging. Wade knew all the driver's energy would be focused on landing a stab or slash. The malicious assailant's arm came down with an overhand thrust, but Wade blocked it and trapped the wrist of the stabbing hand with both of his and smashed the wrist on the truck hood til the knife fell. Wade tripped the driver and shoved him down, to one knee.

"Alright, alright!" the driver shouted.

Wade extended his hand to help the man up, but when they locked hands, he spun it around his back and pressed it above his shoulder blades, causing him to scream. This made it easier to steer him to the ground, where Wade continued applying pressure.

"Was it worth it? Was it worth the three hundred?" Wade shouted as the man screeched in agony.

"I'll give it back!" the man shouted.

"Too late!" Wade seethed as he placed his foot on the man's head and pried his arm upward in a sudden thrust; a loud pop sound was followed by more screaming.

"I'll get you the car!" the man shouted through tears while clutching his arm.

"I don't care anymore," Wade snapped.

"For the love of God, please!" the man desperately begged between whining sounds and tears.

"What would you know of God?"

"That he preaches forgiveness! Now, I'll take you to the car and drive you anyplace you say, and I'll give you your money back as a penance. My arm's broke; I can't fight no more, ya prick! Have some damned humanity!"

"Right, because you always afford people chances."

"Who are you?" the driver asked, widening his gaze.

"I'm not from the part of town where people stop in the middle of a fight."

Wade jabbed him on the bridge of his nose and followed with a left hook to the ribs and an uppercut that opened a blood tap from both nostrils that ran flooding into his goatee, staining his shirt all the way to his belt as he stumbled backward.

"Please! For the love of God, I'm beaten! Look at my arm! I can't even fight back," he shrieked.

Wade was uncertain if it was an overexposure to constantly fighting with people or the pathetic attempt to appeal to religion by someone who clearly never read enough of the Bible to justify his pleas, but he had little interest in fighting an already beaten man sobbing and begging for mercy. Unlike his opponent, Wade didn't believe in targeting the weak or disadvantaged, but his ability to withhold his temper was diminishing, and he knew if he didn't get a handle on it immediately, it would grow monstrous and beyond his control.

"Okay, but if you stick it to me one more time, we're hopscotching it on the stairs. Got it?" Wade spat the words with enough contempt in his voice to invite the driver's desperate expression to wilt into one of tearful moaning and self-pity.

"Alright! But seriously, who the hell are you?" he groaned.

"I'm the son your mother could only wish for," Wade quipped.

After uncovering the hidden vehicle—another Bronco of the same model and color—they drove, only the conversation was more fluid this time. Wade had the driver drop him two streets from The Pitt but ended the conversation on a distinct note.

"Let me see your driver's license; I want to know who messed with me," he said.

The man handed it to him, and he read the name Allan Finch, but it struck no chord of familiarity with him.

"I'm going to have to confiscate your license for a while, Allan, just long enough for you to get a new one. I have a cousin out that way, a real stoner. I was looking for him and got lost. He gets lost sometimes too—not the sharpest shiv in the cell block, you might say. If I ever hear about you taking him for a ride, we're going to have to finish what we started today, you know that, right?" Wade asked.

The driver nodded and sped off without another word.

CHAPTER 11

THE MISSING INGREDIENT

"Stan!" Wade shouted as he saw his friend dressed up as a courier. Instantly, he recognized that Stan was on his way to visit Feland and take action against him. Stan was also pleased to discover Wade was among the living, as they each swung out an arm and clasped hands loudly.

"I gave you an extra day. Once I heard Angel put some herbs in your bag, I looked and noticed she gave you the ones she never lets me use," Stan said, smirking.

"Stop smiling so much, Stan! It makes children nervous," Angel said, causing Stan to smile even wider.

"Here, I saved you a few 'cause I am all done with them forever!" Wade said.

"Hey!" Angel shouted.

Stan snatched them all and ran too fast for anyone to see where he went.

Wade followed Angel into the kitchen to learn more about the herbs and what they might have done to him.

"Angel, I'm about as spiritual as a box of used pop cans, and I don't know what you gave me, but I went over the moon on them. Did I put them in the wrong order or something?"

"Oh, I asked Stan when you were coming back, and he wouldn't give me a straight answer, so I threw in a few extras. I didn't know you had them in a special order or anything. You didn't take too many, I hope, or did you?" Angel asked.

"Well, put it this way: the next time I feel like going for a walk among the dead, I'll call you," Wade joked.

Angel's eyes widened with concern and a little embarrassment as she covered her mouth.

"What did you see?" she asked with her eyes still wide.

"I don't want to trample on anyone's beliefs, but I don't subscribe to the whole idea that hallucinogenics enlighten, talk to God, or reveal solutions to deep-rooted issues, or *any* of the other excuse-to-get-high arguments. I'm sorry if that sounds rude; I just don't buy it," Wade said.

"It's not rude; you believe what you want, but do you mind telling me what you saw?" she asked.

"The dead girl wants me to tell people that the girl in her grave isn't her, and if I am to have any chance with her sister, I need to get on it," Wade said with a shrug.

"Hell of a first trip!" Stan said, returning with an extra wide grin.

"Stan, don't you have some strippers to chase around or some bar fights to start? I'm trying to have a serious conversation here!" Angel said.

"Sure! Wanna come along?" Stan asked.

"What else did you see?" she asked.

"Deneige took a dip in a lake in her birthday suit as the sky and water turned black. That was it," Wade said.

"That's it?" Angel asked.

"Okay, there was a moon that went dark as well, but please don't start reading my tea leaves over this stuff; it holds no value for me," Wade said.

"I won't read your tea leaves, but I can tell you what the dream represents," Angel said.

"Aw, boy!" Wade grimaced.

"The dead girl is the past; the new girl is the future. The black water is power, authority, and great thought—a deeper wisdom. The moon is hope, the lightening of your burdens, and a cleansing of your soul, if you want. All this blackness is linked with the past, and something that went wrong in the past is clouding your judgment and threatening your future—a mistake with an ex-girlfriend, a family member, a broken bond. There is a fear that this will be repeated in the future if you don't corral it. The fact that she was in her birthday suit means you could have a complete life with her if your blackened past doesn't ruin it all for you first. Her request is that you challenge yourself; you'll have a daunting task ahead of you, and I'd say your connection with the spirit world is very strong," Angel said.

"Well, no more herbs for me, okay? Talking dead girls are creepy, and I have enough problems with the living ones on this realm. Thanks just the same," Wade said.

"Maybe it's time to call the princess; you've been gone awhile," Angel said.

"Unghhh!" Wade said.

"Aw, what are you worried about? I know some people on the reservation who'll rent you out a couple of horses for cheap. I'll get Gayle to drive them out here for ya. Take her out horseback riding. Girls love that! Do you want me to wine and dine her for you too? She's mad at you, so what? Get off your ass and take her out!" Angel insisted.

The next day, the horses were dropped off, and Deneige reluctantly agreed to meet him, but the horses clinched the deal. They rode along a remote highway until they found the first dirt road that was blocked off by a lopsided metal sign that read "No Trespassing," but Deneige's horse, Archie, ran toward the fence and leaped over it in perfect form. Wade's horse, Slider, tensed up, ready to sprint, and after it became clear Deneige's horse had no intention of turning back, Slider followed and just barely cleared the fence. Archie ran wild, and Wade had no choice but to follow as they passed a mill and a river before Archie would rest. Deneige dismounted aher fatigued steed let him feed untended.

"This is fun, but I just wanted to tell you in person that I really can't see you anymore," Deneige said.

"You have good reason, but I'd still like the chance to make my case," Wade said.

"You are a brooding, semi-violent outcast with really far-out ideas, and you show little regard for social norms or even common courtesy. That's just not something I can really deal with in my life, and my parents aren't perfect, but I am not going to date someone who is at odds with them indefinitely. I hope you understand," Deneige said.

"Yes, I do, but there is more to the story," Wade said.

"You mean you are more violent, more of an outcast, or more disrespectful of social norms?"

"Let's start at the beginning: when we met, there were certain impulses that drove us toward each other. Now, you are a stunning vision of what other women only hope to be. You are smart, emotionally together, gorgeous, and refined. It's a lot to contend with, and the reason most men don't ask you out isn't your parents; it's the intimidation factor. You need someone who isn't insecure and won't be envious of the attention you get. You'll need someone who can protect you from the creeps that will undoubtedly scheme to take advantage of you. This is the reason your parents finally approved of someone for you. They may be highly pissed with me at this moment, but let's not lose sight of the fact that the two people you trust most granted their approval of me. They felt I was the best choice of anyone you've ever brought home. Then there is your part: you used your advanced social skills to make the path easier for me because you knew I was taken with you. I could barely think straight around you. This is not the first time this has happened, I'm sure, but that's not your fault. You didn't behave this way to dump me a few days in or just to test the waters. The reason I know you care for me is that, despite the fact that you are beautiful and I'm reasonable-looking, you seek strength and character—someone who will keep their word no matter what the risk is. Embarrassment, offending your darling's parents, ostracizing friends—the truth will prevail. If you doubt me, I'll hand you some more truth because it comes easily to me. I'm not semi-violent; I am completely violent. This is because certain occasions not only call for it, they demand it. I've never hit a girl in my life because I'm not a coward. You find one of the smooth, non-violent types and ask them how they get it out of their systems, then hope it doesn't take the form of a kink you can't come back from. Yes, your folks are pissed with me, but it's because I couldn't bring myself to lie to them, and that is the only reason. I care more about you than anyone I have had in my entire life! So, if you are going to take out your knife and stab this emerging love between us at its infancy while it is ballooning into something more powerful than either of us, just to please your parents, then stab away. Just realize you aren't just cutting away at me, but yourself and your future as well. I'll be here for you if you change your mind," Wade said.

"I asked you not to talk to them about her, and you ignored me," Deneige said.

"I made a horrible choice, trying to do the right thing, and I might lose you over it."

"You are wanting a second chance after what you've said?"

"More than anything," he said.

"What about my parents?" she asked.

"We'll give them a bit of time to heal, and then tell them I started calling you again."

"You mean sneak around? Isn't that the same as lying?" she asked.

"Yes, but if it means seeing you again, I'd put my hand on a hot stove element. I'm crazy over you," he said.

"Maybe just crazy?"

"You're still here; I couldn't have said anything that crazy!" Wade said, grinning.

"You're a bit of a cocky bastard, aren't you?"

"Well, maybe if we knew a nice, refined girl with elegant manners and city polish, she could teach an outcast a thing or two about etiquette. What do you say?"

"I'd say next time don't warn me about smooth talkers; it's counter-productive for you," Deneige smiled.

"Your horse has run off; we'd better make hay!"

Deneige lurched forward and pushed him to the ground without warning, then stood over him, laughing.

"You, my dear, have a latent violent streak!" Wade said.

"Wanna fight? I used to be a tomboy when I was young; I'll have you know," she said.

"In the street, I could take you, but strict-rules wrestling, who knows?" Wade said.

They wrestled, they played, and then they were carelessly intimate, leaving clothes strewn all over the field. They explored each other's bodies with patience and passion until Deneige's horse eventually returned. Darkness fell, and Deneige called her mother while Wade retrieved their clothes.

"For a segregated damsel locked away in an ivory tower, you are pretty wild," Wade said.

"Think of me as the ink stain on your Rorschach test; next time you have one," she grinned.

A weathered-looking woman on a horse, with one hand on the reins and the other holding a double-barreled shotgun, rode up to them with a stupefied look on her face.

"Now, what in the devil's armpit brought you two here?" she asked.

Wade, still putting his shirt on, offered only a sheepish grin. Deneige tied her hair back and said nothing.

"Well, I don't see any knapsacks, so you didn't come here to steal anything; I don't see any weapons, so it's not a stick-up; and I don't see anyone who likes keeping their clothes on either. What are you, freaks or something? You trespass on private property just so you can get it on? Is that it?" she asked, still looking more perplexed than angry.

"No, we rented horses for the first time, and my unruly horse jumped your fence, and then took off on me, so Wade followed, until we were stranded and left to our own devices," Deneige said.

"What kind of devices? I don't see any devices. Do you mean cameras?" the woman asked.

"I meant we indulged our affections," Deneige clarified.

"Oh well, yeah, I gathered that much, and I don't want to disturb you gentle people, but what the hell are you doing here? You couldn't find a motel or something? Hell's Bells!" she said.

"We'll leave immediately, and we're sorry for the indiscretion; there's no excuse," Wade said.

"No manners on ya, huh?"

"We are very sorry," Wade confirmed.

"No, I didn't mean that, but now that you're here, you might as well come back to the house for a drink. I'm Marge, and I don't get many visitors out this way, and those horses are going to be too tired to drag you back 'cause I can tell you aren't from around here," she said.

Wade and Deneige looked at each other and shrugged.

"Sure, I'm Deneige, and that's a very kind gesture, Marge," she said.

"And thanks for not pointing the gun at us," Wade added.

Once at the house, Wade passed on the drink, while the two women tilted a few back and exchanged some lighthearted laughs.

"Well, if you don't bring those horses back, you'll get charged an arm and a leg," Marge said.

"I guess so," he said.

"These rental horses follow each other around like squirrels; why don't you bring them back, and I'll keep your girlfriend company with some girl talk until you return? I'd drive her home, but I've had a couple too many. Don't worry, she'll be alright here with me, won'tcha, Deneige?"

Wade scanned her face to detect any deception or ill will, but saw only creases from overused smile lines and lifelines that grew out of her crow's feet. He hadn't studied her baseline expressions enough to determine if she was hiding something.

"Sure, Wade, I'll be fine. The shotgun's been put away, and we're having too pleasant a time to cut it short. You can call the guys to pick me up when you dump off the horses, and Margie here, can drop me off in the morning if she feels up to it, and if not, you can come get me," Deneige said.

"Sure, it's just that I'm the sort of guy who leaves the dance with the girl I arrived with, and we can't impose on Marge here by using her as a taxi service; after we trespassed on her property like that, I couldn't live with myself," he said.

"Oh, nonsense! I'd be thrilled to drive your lovely girlfriend home tomorrow, and I've got extra bacon and eggs for breakfast in the morning; it'd be my pleasure," Marge said.

"Wade, it's fine; I'm a big girl. There are enough dogs on and around the property to protect us, and I don't need a third parent. I'll be fine," Deneige said.

"I think I've been outvoted," Wade said.

"If she misses you, she can call you on her cell phone," Marge said.

"Wade hates cell phones. He says they leak radiation, and loves to point out that it even says so on your legal agreement when you purchase one. That was enough for him, but he loses out on convenience," Deneige said.

"If you read the legal section of your user agreement, you'll find that they advise you not to keep one in your pocket. Why? Because of leaking radiation, and when does it leak the most? When you say hello—that's when the charge blasts forward and you get jacked full of radiation—but maybe you folks enjoy that, or maybe you don't like to read. Now, you wouldn't mind calling Jake to meet me on the reservation, would you?" Wade asked.

"Sure, oh, my battery is dead. I guess that's a no-go," Deneige said.

"That's why you should always get a cell phone, because they are so great in emergencies, right?" Wade asked.

"Please forgive him, Marge; he gets a little paranoid at night sometimes," Deneige said.

"Well, I can see why. I mean, he has this elegant, regal-looking woman, and he's probably worried he might lose you one day. Men today can be so disappointing in all sorts of ways—nothing personal toward you, of course—but may I ask what you do for work?" Marge asked.

"Odd jobs, really odd jobs," Deneige said, laughing.

"I help people in trouble and sometimes deal with missing persons, Marge. Has anybody around here ever gone missing mysteriously? I hope that's not a sore topic or anything," Wade asked.

"I'm sorry, Wade; I didn't mean to make fun of your work. That was out of line," Deneige said.

"The only thing that sucks about it is that on rare occasions you end up having to work for the same household twice," Wade said.

"Wade, I'm sorry, I crossed a line, but I'm not about to go missing and have been taking care of myself quite well for years now," Deneige said.

"No, it's fine. Tell someone you just met all about me, and make sure you give her my social security number, just in case she has to do some checking. I've got some horses to tend to," he said, and left without waiting for a response.

CHAPTER 12

A BRIEF CASE

A week later, after a hiatus, Deneige called Wade, breaking the stubbornness contest.

"Hey, I have some news. The police contacted my folks with a heap of apologies, and it looks like there was no conspiracy, but rather a simple mix-up regarding the DNA. You were right the whole time; my family was provided with the wrong person's remains," she said.

"Imagine!" Wade said.

"It's terrible news, but there will be an exhumation, and some compensation will be coming for my parents. They feel badly over the way they treated you," she said.

"Tell them there is no harm done and no need for concern; our business is concluded, and I wish them closure and inner peace," he said.

"And what about me?" Deneige asked.

"I wish you closure and inner peace as well."

"That's not what I meant, and you know it," she said.

"If you need questions answered, I'll be busily carousing with my fellow outcasts; call anytime," he said.

"Wait, one more thing. The old lady wasn't a threat, but she did try to get a little amorous with me, so all I did was talk about you all night, and then she couldn't wait to get rid of me. She wasn't a true threat per se, but you were right; people often have hidden agendas, and I gave my trust away too easily, and that could have turned out badly. I've come to realize a few things about you that I was wrong about," she said.

"All's forgiven," Wade said.

"I've told my folks that we're seriously involved, and they are okay with it," Deneige added.

"So, I am back on the good Scotch and macaroons list, then?"

"That's not fair; they've been through a lot," she said.

"Okay, it's all fine. Call me tonight; I have to resolve something here first," Wade said and hung up.

He went to the lounge area of The Pitt to find Angel and Suzette watching black-and-white movies.

"What are you watching?" Wade asked.

"A double feature: Dracula and The Bride of Frankenstein," Angel said.

"It's a documentary about Stan's parents," Suzette added.

Stan tipped his head in acknowledgement. Wade beckoned Suzette with his finger, indicating he required a private word, and she followed him into the kitchen.

"I am going to ask you something that'll sound weird, but can you humor me with it? Deneige's parents got word that they got the wrong body from the cops. That's not the sort of mistake they would usually make. Did you put a call through to someone, forge a document, lure someone into providing a DNA folder, or anything like that?" Wade asked.

"Nope, I didn't think we were still dealing with any of that—nothing at all," Suzette said.

"Do you find it odd?" he asked.

"Well, the troubling thing about human error is that it can happen on any level, even where it should never happen. You can't always assume hostility when random error, clumsiness, oversights, or plain old stupidity might be to blame," she said.

"A fluke!"

"Maybe, or not, I'm just saying I was nowhere near this one," Suzette said.

Angel took a phone call, wrote down some details after asking some questions, and hung up the phone looking proud.

"Guys, we've got a case! A real case. This guy, Mr. Craven, says he wants us to investigate a makeshift burial ground and see if his missing daughter disappeared near there. He is in a wheelchair, so he can't do it. He'll give us five grand for a yes or no answer. We just check it out," she said.

"Sounds fishy!" Jake said.

"For five grand, we could check it out," Stan said.

"He sounded legit, as far as I could tell over the phone," Angel said.

"I dunno. Wade gets all into deep-dive mode with this dead chick and her sister, then there's all this weird stuff with a casket and remains, and now someone calls us up five minutes after it's resolved, asking us to check out something so similar in nature that there's almost no chance of us saying no to it. From an outside point of view, and to me, it sounds like a setup," Jake said.

"Are we getting too paranoid to even take on cases now?" Suzette asked.

"It seems to me that being paranoid saved our asses more than a few times," Ray said.

"The best way to spring a trap is to get a closer look," Wade said.

"Let's get the money in advance as a test; if they pay it with no questions asked, it's definitely a setup," Stan said.

"My guess is they'll press us to go look in a hurry, and then they'll know when to expect us there and show up armed behind our backs," Ray said.

"Am I the only one thinking this might be unrelated to anything and completely random?" Suzette said.

Angel placed a call to Mr. Craven, explaining that due to the risks, the fee would be required in advance and paid in cash. She was told that he'd send a private courier with half the sum, or no deal. About 30 minutes later, a woman dressed like a courier arrived. She was invited in, and she took off her hat and jacket, smiling widely and gushing with enthusiasm. She had a pretty face and a buxom body with bronze skin that drew the attention of all. She shook everyone's hand and laughed warmly and easily whenever she spoke. Brenda had pretty eyes too and exquisitely shaped white teeth that made for a natural smile that just lit up the room. She handed the money to Angel and did not ask for a receipt.

"I'm Brenda, and I'm a huggerrrrr!" she said, extending her arms toward Angel.

"Oh, awright then," Angel said while offering a skeptical sideward glance.

Brenda made a miniature hopping motion and proceeded to hug each member of the group, smiling widely each time.

"We've been overdue for a little added cheer and positivity. Who ever knew all it would take was someone with a decent disposition to help us get our groove back?" Ray asked.

"So what do you do when you aren't making deliveries?" Suzette asked.

"Well, I tried my hand at singing, but I wasn't too good, and I dated a guy in the military, so we stayed in Germany for two years, where he got stationed. We broke up though, so now I'm kind of starting all over again, at the beginning, but it was great meeting all of you," she said.

"Auf Wiedersehen," Stan said.

"I'm fine! How are you?" she replied, wide-eyed and smiling appreciatively.

The entire room was grinning.

"Anyways, I should run, but it was really lovely meeting you all! Maybe we'll see each other around," Brenda said, and she left.

"Well, she sure seemed nice," Ray said.

"I liked her too," Jake said.

"See, not everyone is a chameleon with hidden machinations. Are you guys willing to admit you were wrong?" Suzette asked.

"Even Stan was trying to pick her up with the two words he knows in German," Jake said, laughing.

"Yup, and when I said goodbye to her in German, she told me she was fine, and all I can say about her is that she's never spent five seconds in Germany," Stan said, cutting through the room-wide enthusiasm.

"Why say it then?" Wade asked.

"Maybe she was in jail and needs a good cover story," Angel said.

"Or in a cult," Jake added.

"So, why are the lines blurring here? Wade's over his dead-girl hang-up, and no one is actually working on a case, so who is feeling threatened enough to keep sending people after us?" Suzette asked.

"If all roads go through Feland, let's make him do something rash and clumsy when he's mad," Jake said.

"He's not one to panic, so we'll have to be cautious," Wade said.

"I'll show up an hour late at the place he told Angel to send us. They should be gone by then, and we can go back at night and see if it's anything like Craven said," Jake said.

"Maybe somebody still wants the dead girl's sister, besides Wade, that is," Ray said.

"Her name's Melanie, not 'the dead girl,' and Deneige said she hasn't noticed anything weird lately beyond the wayward affections of an old farm lady," Wade said.

Two hours later, Jake came back with a report, and Stan said he'd sent Feland a friendly message from Craven in case they were working together.

"There are two properties; one looks like a small old mansion that's been modernized by blending it with an administration building. That's the draw, but I had to drive a good way around the perimeter to notice the property behind it on the other side of the fence. It's all boarded up, but it's got similar architecture without the updated touches. In these parts, wealthy families used to secure properties near each other and try to marry off their kids so they wouldn't mix blood with the common folk. You know, like us, probably," Jake said with a grin.

"And?" Ray asked impatiently.

"That second property is huge and boarded up something fierce. No wandering vagrant is getting inside that place without a key, a crowbar, and a formal invitation. In fact, the more I looked at it, I kept wondering why so much effort went into boarding up a property, and I kept wondering if it wasn't just to keep people out, but also to keep people in!" Jake said.

"Can you be sure about that, Jake?" Stan asked.

"As sure as most people will cross the street whenever they see you coming," Jake said.

"I think we're all going to have to check this place out tonight. Bring penlights; if people see flashlight beams moving around, we'll be stopped at the driveway and have to explain ourselves," Wade said.

That evening, at 10:30 PM, they drove up to the adjacent properties with the Jeep after having coated the license plate with mud that was now nearly baked on, for stealth. Stan had found out that Feland's first name was Lorne and couriered a gift-wrapped golf club to him as a symbol of Wade's warning and to advise him that they knew where he resided. They had addressed it as being from Noel Feland, and despite the enticement from one of Stan's stripper friends toward the courier, they still had to overpay for the 10 minutes of vehicle and uniform privilege.

Their destination was an old Victorian-style mansion with white walls and columns supporting its balconies, and while it could have used a coat of paint on the exterior, it still had an impressively regal air about it.

"Why is the fence in such good condition if the front gates are wide open?" Ray asked.

"You can't maintain the illusion of it being a dilapidated old relic with a new electronic fence like the one across the yard," Wade said.

"I checked the gateway, and it seems fine, but I'll keep the engine running across the street; if you have problems, shine your light right at the Jeep, and I'll floor it and get you out," Jake said.

"Hold it! There is a sensor mike right there in the grass, about ten feet in from the pavement," Stan said.

"Okay, Wade, and I will check the building for a way in, but Stan, you better clear the grounds for us first and point out the exit route when we come out," Ray said.

"You mean, if you come out, I'll circle the area and clear any other mikes. They aren't cameras, so as long as they don't hear me disconnecting them, it should be alright, and then I'll follow you in," Stan said.

"Why wouldn't they use cameras?" Ray asked.

"Same as the fence, an old condenser mike could be left lying around on an abandoned property. They're battery-powered, so there's no way to tell who's listening on the other end or even if anyone is listening. If it's discovered, someone keeps or tosses it without a second thought. You put in CCTV, and everyone knows it's not abandoned, and it's cheaper as well. There's probably only one or two in place, but someone is definitely paying attention to what goes on here," Jake said.

"Like maybe the folks with the electric fence that runs through the backyard?" Wade asked.

After perusing the perimeter of the property and finding the doubled boards over the windows had been secured with both nails and screws, Ray silently signalled a find tilting his head toward a small window frame that was missing a bottom corner screw. It was still nailed, but they the first board could be pulled free. The two men lodged their fingers around the final board's base and began rocking their weights to and fro in unison to loosen the board. They had no desire to be caught on private property with anything that could be deemed an offensive weapon by the police, so there were no hammers, crowbars, or bats on this trip.

The sound of splintering wood could be heard at first on Wade's side, then Ray's, before the entire slab fell from the window frame. The thick wooden panel was much larger than the small window frame it protected, reinforcing the idea of imprisoning any occupants rather than deterring outsiders.

Wade lifted Ray onto his shoulders, helping him inside. Ray popped his head out a moment later, looking frustrated.

"It's dark as fuck in here. It's like ink! I can't see my hand, even with the penlight. It's weirdly dark in this place!" he whispered.

"Just go find the front door and open it!" Wade said.

The minutes ticked by on his watch as Wade grew distressed over the delay, until he found Stan to help him up into the window. Elbow-walking across the window frame with his penlight in his mouth, Wade sensed he was in a kitchen. The window offered scant illumination, and the penlight seemed more like a lit cigarette in a row boat at night. Wade was pretty comfortable in the dark, as he felt it was an equal disadvantage to an enemy. The darkness in here, however, felt different; it hung in the air like a pure black fog. Once his ribs and hips passed the frame, he fell forward from quite a drop but rolled out of it until he landed against a wall. Wade allowed himself a moment for his eyes to adjust, as many nights spent in the woods or on the streets had given him an education in seeing fragmented light and shadows within the shadows. On this night, however, he only detected a rancid odor like that of a foul-smelling animal doused with incense. He knew his penlight would only serve as a signal for an enemy to find him instantly, while any foe remained unseen beyond the overlapping layers of dense blackness. He switched his light off, knowing better than to remain where his light was last seen. Blindly feeling the walls for a way to the next corridor, his foot struck a solid, heavy object like a metal crate or a stack of skids. He put his forearm to his mouth to smother the sound he knew might give his position away. He put his shoes around his fists and trotted silently down a hall in his socks, running with his elbow just grazing the wall for a sense of surroundings. He heard sounds from upstairs; a chain rattled and clinked, and he sensed the full weight of a large body was shambling around above him somewhere.

Standing still, this belly of blackness betrayed no sense of light coming through any crevices, no rough shapes in shadow among the ever-present, all-encompassing passage that swallowed all light. It was as though someone had painted fresh tar across his eyes. Once he felt sure no one could guess his whereabouts, he put his shoes back on, grateful they bore no laces. More sounds came from upstairs, with more movement of bodies shifting around, muffled by their whispers. Wade felt around for window frames or anything he could pry free to use as a weapon.

Ray had been searching for the foyer at the main entrance of the building. It seemed obvious at first, but the interior felt different than what he'd imagined, and he was staggering around like a blind fool. Then at last he found the main foyer, and by his penlight he could just barely make out the front doors and spiraling staircases on either side of the room, but the center of it was entirely black and was the source of an unbearably foul smell. Even with his light pointed right at this darkened area, he could only make out the general shape as he realized, one second too late, that he was standing over a cavernous pit. There was a toxic mixture of vomit-inducing odors: urine, decay, lime, phosphorous, and dead animals. He wasn't sure what he was lying on when he landed from the fall and propped himself up on a pile of unknown contents where the worst of the odors were emitting. With his sleeve over his face, he started searching for a way up to the unseen doors.

Wade didn't know it, but he was on the other side of the building and had found himself by a set of side stairs that led upward but not down to the basement. If they'd caught Ray, and if it was half as dark up there, they'd mistake him for one of theirs, and he might have an advantage. The stairs creaked noisily, however, all but begging to expose him, as he kept his feet to the outer edge of each step, avoiding the creaky centers. He felt for a door handle and squeezed it tightly with one hand, and gently pulled it outward with the other, so it might turn silently. The door opened as he stared into the ominous black, but a slow, high-pitched whiny creak of the hinges betrayed his presence as he felt numerous hands clutch him at once, pulling him violently to the ground.

"It's a Keeper!" A female voice hissed across the unforgiving darkness as he fell backward.

He received punches, kicks, and scratches from jagged fingernails, as human teeth bit into his left bicep and just over his right knee before he could get up.

"How do you like it, Keeper?" an unseen male voice cried with glee from no particular direction.

The jeers, howls, and grunts grew louder in the dark, but not as loud as the silence of a held breath before an attack. Wade didn't like being the house special on the menu, and his temper erupted. He grabbed onto one of the wrists from the hands clutching at him and bent it awkwardly, as a voice piercingly shrieked in reaction. He clenched one finger in his other hand and forced it all the way to the back of a wrist. It snapped, and he repeated this action four times so quickly that he almost forgot his purpose and went completely berserk. Swinging and clutching wildly at anything he could get a grip on, he furiously attacked any sound he heard in the hall. He grabbed an arm, guessed at the location of its skull, and head-butted it viciously three times in rapid succession. This produced no outcry, but he heard the body collapse to the ground with a thud and a voiceless bounce, undoubtedly concussed. He heard another body shifting its weight, and he jumped at it with a leaping side kick that landed chest-high, and another body went toppling in the dark. Wade swung his fists angrily but hit only air, and he detected vague gasps and groans from his new hosts. He grabbed at the next bit of breathing he heard and felt a neck in his hands.

"Who are you?" Wade hollered, blind in vision and with rage.

"I don't know," the voice said.

"Who the fuck are you?" Wade screamed at the robed body.

"We don't know much," the voice said.

"I'll snap your neck like a twig if you don't tell me," Wade said with a calm chill in his voice.

"They call me 'Poodle' sometimes," he said.

A cold sweat came over Wade as he sensed no deception in the young man's voice. Indications of what he'd just endured dawned on him. These were the cult's tortured victims who'd attacked him; they had to have taken him to be a careless guard, and they saw their moment for retribution literally in the dark. He now had to live with his mistaking them for active cultists, just as they had mistook him as one of their captors.

"Where are the lights in here?" Wade asked.

"No lights, never," a female voice said.

"I need to apologize to those people," he said.

"We've all been through it so many times; it's fine," she said.

"It's not fine, and I'm getting you people out of here! My friend Ray is in here too. I have to find him."

"Sounds like he fell in the pit; I'll take you," a female voice said.

Wade felt some reluctance to go to a place called "the pit" if his friend fell in, thinking he might be next.

"What's in the pit?" he asked.

"That's where they put our pets if we don't please them," the female voice said.

A host of images ran through Wade's mind as the enormity of the cruelty going on within these walls struck him.

"Okay, look, we're all getting out of here tonight! Some people might be too scared, and while we can't force them, they should know that when the Keepers come back, they'll probably kill them. I need you to convince everyone in here to meet me by the front doors once I get Ray out of the pit. Everyone! Okay?"

Wade said it in the kindest voice he could manage, but the perpetrators of these crimes against humanity had lit a fire inside him, and he was all but lusting for revenge.

The chains locked, the push handles on the front doors trembled once or twice, and the sound of an engine revving in the distance could be heard just seconds before the front door on the left came flying off its hinges, and the supporting chains snapped and fell to the ground in a heap. Stan and Jake had secured their own chain and hook to the door handle and used the Jeep's momentum to rip it from its partner. Stan climbed through the doorway, waving his penlight high and low.

"Here!" Wade yelled.

"Where?" Stan called out.

"Ray's stuck in that pit; use that chain. I'll get Jake to shine his headlights in, but we've got to get out of here!"

Stan was all set to pull Ray up, but he mounted the chain and climbed out faster than expected.

"Whoa, you smell worse than the fish we gave those holy rollers back in the day! I heard your new hit song on the radio; what's it called again? 'The Outhouse Blues'?" Stan asked.

"Never mind, we have got a dozen victims in there who haven't seen sunlight, maybe in years," Ray said.

One by one, they came staggering out of the door frame, squinting as they looked up, shielding their eyes, and looking lost. In robes or rags, most were pale, underfed, and perplexed at the open space. There were nine in total, one with broken fingers, and the Jeep only seated four.

"What are we going to do with them at this hour?" Stan asked.

"They can't stay here; they'll just get scooped up again," Wade said.

"The odor is an issue; we can't bring them to a restaurant or hotel. Should we bring them back to The Pitt?" Ray asked.

"Not the pit! No! No pit!" several protest shouts rang out at once.

"It's not that kind of pit; it's sort of a lounge area we hang out at. It's a converted loft," Ray said.

"No pit! No Way!" a pale, black-haired girl shrieked.

Jake came out of the mansion, swearing. He'd gone in to satisfy his curiosity and came out shouting.

"Those miserable subhuman assholes! There was a kid asleep in that pit, and that's where they put them to punish them, the scumbags! If I get my hands on one of them, you'll see me on the news! Just wait!"

"We'll have to call social services; there's kids in there," Wade said.

"What if they have the sort of connections to find them through the system?" Ray asked.

"Ray, you take the Jeep and get a few of them to the reservation; you can reach Mrs. Moran there. She's a bit of a medicine woman, kind of a spiritual healer; she'll have better ideas than any of us. Besides, I want to be here if any of those clowns show up," Jake said.

"Their eyes haven't adjusted yet; we should split. They won't be able to identify anyone right now, and we could get picked up for breaking and entering. There was a confused fight in the dark that could mean assault charges. The guys who run these things are going to come at us with all they've got; we *cannot* hang around. Send them down the street, and we'll make a pickup spot for Ray. If we stay here, we're all in front of a judge in the morning," Stan said.

The three friends walked with malnourished and confused followers, powered only by the exuberance of being outside for the first time in years. The group was so worn down that they were just happy to turn right or left based on their own free will. Jake was concerned that the street offered little cover in case of trouble, but by 4:30 AM, Ray had made enough trips to bring all of these domestic refugees to safety and finally collected his pals, who slept in cramped positions in the Jeep.

CHAPTER 13

Boiling Frog Bravado

Jake had been making regular trips to the reservation and enduring anguished tales about a torture room that had a chair with bindings that sat in the center. It was a well-lit room surrounded by Plexiglass and had two rows of elevated viewing chairs that someone in charge could entertain guests in. Wade pondered what sort of clientele would eagerly watch real torture take place at the hands of a hooded henchman for a fee. The chair also served as a motivator for those with thoughts of leaving the order. The doubter would be placed in the chair after having just viewed a human being brought to their limits of screaming, begging, and finally silence, as they either passed out or succumbed to their injuries. The doubter would be given one last chance to change their mind after being strapped in, and the man in charge would offer a change of heart if they could count on the doubter's loyalty. This often instilled the most zealous levels of loyalty and subservience.

"We have to go back there!" Jake announced to the group at The Pitt.

Deneige was visiting and had been attending to some of the younger victims at the reservation and spending more time at The Pitt with Wade where tensions were rising.

"How long has this been going on for?" she asked.

"First of all, those people—if you can call them that—deserve to die, and secondly, we have to find the tunnel to the other building and find that chair room. We dismantle it and call the cops on them," Jake said.

"Okay, but this time, we're bringing mega-lumen torch lights and nose guards," Ray said.

"You're not sending the cops?" Deneige asked.

"We're short on proof; the victims are here on the reservation, and the cops have no jurisdiction on this land. They can't even show up without permission, which is rarely granted," Suzette said.

"The creeps kept them uneducated, abused, and intimidated. They might not be ready to be jumped by high-priced lawyers and the system before we've even found them proper homes," Ray said.

"So you're just going to take the law into your own hands and do what exactly?" Deneige asked.

"Look, they aren't going in as an execution squad; they are going to rock their world a little, that's all," Suzette said.

"It wouldn't take much for me to be talked into heading an execution squad right now," Jake said.

"Let's keep our heads cool," Wade said.

"Yeah, we wouldn't want to go off on a tirade and start breaking random people's fingers or anything," Jake said.

"I got jumped in the darkest pitch of black we've ever seen. What the hell would you have done? You're half ready to go on a killing spree right now!" Wade said.

"Alright, yes! I want to go in there, busting heads apart and leaving bodies sprawled on the ground. There, I said it!" Jake shouted.

"What is he talking about, broken fingers?" Deneige asked.

"I was being bitten and clawed in the dark, so I lashed out, and things got messy," Wade said.

"You attacked those enslaved victims?" Deneige asked in horror.

"No, they attacked me, and I defended myself," Wade said.

"By breaking their fingers? I saw that young man, and he has four broken fingers. What were you thinking after you broke the first one? 'Hey, I've got three more to go. This is fun; maybe you'll never write again'?" Deneige said.

Wade pulled off his shirt, revealing deep red claw marks on his chest and multicolored bruising on welts that came from human mouths clamping down on his skin. Only his clothing prevented the bites from breaking through the skin. Everyone stepped back, and they grew quiet once they'd seen the damage he endured.

"Maybe we should all cut you some slack, seeing as we weren't the first ones in there," Jake said.

"You could apologize, too, Deneige, that is, if you want to," Angel said.

"No one has to apologize; they thought I was a cult leader, I thought they were too, everyone went hell-bent for leather, and it was over in a few seconds. It was mass regrets all the way around," Wade said.

"No one wants to see these people punished more than I do, but don't you see what is happening?" Deneige asked indignantly.

"Tell us," Stan said sarcastically.

"You are getting worse and worse! You started out as cult rescuers, freeing victims; then you became cult hunters, finding out where they roost and how to get them by any means necessary. Con them, get them arrested, beat them up, shake them down—anything to satisfy your hell-bent lust for vengeance. Where would you all be if not for this shady work? In jail, working for the mob as leg-breakers? Sorry, finger-breakers? What's become of you all? You are constantly sidestepping the police. You are plotting extreme tactics with increasing regularity, and you are going to do the same things the cults do: break people down and leave them a shell of what they were meant to be. This is vigilantism, and it happens to be a crime, and is illegal for a reason. The minute you give yourselves permission to brutalize someone at will, you are doing exactly what the cults do!" she persisted.

"So we should just let the authorities handle it then? And how's that going so far? How much did it help your sister?" Stan asked.

"That's enough!" Angel said.

"Well, she didn't answer, did she? Her boyfriend's all carved up like a half-eaten birthday cake, and all she can do is tell us what bad people we are," Jake said.

"Leave her sister out of it," Suzette said.

"Deneige and I are going to go off and see if we can sort this stuff out between us, alone," Wade said.

There was a knock at the door, and all eyes took turns scanning each other for any indication of who it might be. Stan got up and opened the door, surprised to see the punk that Ray had pummeled into submission and choked out in the baseball cage.

"Hey, I'm 'ere to see Ray. I wanted to make our peace a bit and tell him 'good fight.' Is 'e here?"

"I'm here!" Ray barked, expecting a second round with his adversary.

"Naw, naw, it's not like that; I've nevuh had a beatdown like that before, and nevuh given one where the guy kept comin'. When did ya know you had me? And what kept ya goin'? I thought you wuz the livin' dead or somefin'; you fought a hell of a fight!" he said.

"What happened to you?" Ray asked.

"Ah, well, me mates heard the sirens, left me there, and ran for it. Most of 'em got caught an' deported to various places around Europe. I went back the facto' to heal up, but finally I had to hit a hospital, an' tol' 'em I got rolled in an alleyway and lost me wallet in the process. You broke me orbital bone, and they still wouldn't touch me wivout insurance. Then some religious wankuh comes up to me and says, 'Nevuh fear, me son, nevuh fear!' and this tossuh paid me medical bills, right there! They put a piece of metal in me orbital bone, and I had to sit still as all hell for days, but now I'm right as rain. I was just goin' to come by an' offuh a congratulations to the toughest guy I've evuh fought, but there's somefin' else," he said.

"Come in and have a seat," Ray said.

"Yesterday, some freepio come sniffin' about, lookin' at our place, which is empty now, then lookin' at your place an' gets on 'eez celly and starts barkin' out the orders like 'eez General Patton, 'cept it was in German, or Czech or somefin'. Now, I din' wanna to get nicked for squattin', so I ditched on the fly. So I'm watchin' from a roof for sirens, but instead I see a dark Humvee turn up wiv four guys in it, all dressed in fatigues."

"Sorry, a freepio?" Suzette asked.

"That's a guy in a three-piece suit. Go ahead," Stan said.

"Yeah, these guys split off inna two groups, right? And there's one wankuh lyin' down in the grass an' 'eez got one of 'em lyin'-down machine guns wiv a belt o' bullets across it. An' he pulls a blanket made of grass ovuh 'eez head, an' 'ee only reason you could spot him was that the grass was slightly greener than wot we got here. Now his partner starts walkin' up to your door, an' I'm like, where's 'ee uhvuh two? Then I look around an' a little further back on 'ee uhvuh side, and one's lyin' down wiv a long rifle, all scoped up an' wotnot, while 'ee uhvuh guy is playing with some weird devices, talkin' to him."

"A Browning," Stan said.

"What?" Angel asked.

"That machine gun is for heavy duty. They were looking to take us all out in one go. In case people scatter in too many different directions for the sniper, the side gunner picks off the trash," Stan said.

"What else?" Ray asked.

"You were very brave, four of you, standin' up to a mob of us—kudos—and while I'd love to stay an' chat, this place is a bit of a target, an' I'm in no shape to fuck wif the military. So, I don't know whose breakfast you pissed in, but it wasn't us; those blokes are well outside our paygrade, ya know?"

With that, he shook Ray's hand and called him a hell of a scrapper, and after being thanked profusely by all, he left. Any philosophical disagreements were quickly forgotten, as the very walls seemed to be ticking time bombs. The idea of darting away into the path of a sniper's bullet served as a sobering wake-up call.

"A show of hands for anyone who thinks he's lying? ...No? Anyone think he was put up to do this?" Jim asked.

"He wasn't very focused on convincing us, and there were a lot of little details a fabrication typically wouldn't have," Suzette said.

"Those highly trained guys don't need a tip-off to mess with their plans. They are all about precision and getting in and out in record time. They don't play games like that," Wade said.

"So, how do we use this to our advantage?" Ray asked.

"We light a fire next door in the abandoned factory, call 911, and say we think there's squatters in there. Then we move our stuff while the fire trucks are here; it's our best shot," Wade said.

"I'll go. I'm the smallest target, and I'll bring Riley for protection, and there's no reason to shoot a dog if they just want to kill us," Angel said.

"Look at you guys! Somebody's freakin' army is here to kill us all, and your temperatures don't even rise? Just another day at the office? Are you all insane? This stops now! That's it, or you are all dead! Do you think if you sneak away from them this time, they will just call it a day and say, 'Oh well,' like it was an unlucky try at fishing? They will track you, stalk you, and kill you—dead! Then they will have experts come in to clean up the mess! Bits of you all are going to end up being served in gourmet restaurants! Wake up!" Deneige implored.

Riley didn't like her tone and started growling at her, so Wade put him in the other room.

"These things require careful tactics, but I'll tell you this much: if we are careless, if we panic, or pack up and run, we will be in the cult's service just like those victims we freed in no time flat. There is someone pulling the strings to get those assassins—or soldiers of fortune—after us. If we get to him, then we can cut those strings and cancel the contract. Any other method gets us killed or made into cult slaves," Wade said.

"You proud little monkeys think this is some kind of game. Those mercenaries are trained killers! They are going to drop you in your tracks from five hundred feet away! They have probably already figured out all your plans. How many of you have any military training—any of you? Not even one? Do you think a black belt in street fighting is going to offset a sniper and his best friends? You've all gone mad!" Deneige protested.

"If they can figure out we'd go to Feland, or Craven, or whoever else is behind this, wouldn't they also be able to anticipate escape routes like bus stations, airports, and car rentals? Running only makes their job that much easier," Wade said.

"So, what do we do then?" Suzette asked.

"Grab everything you need and only what will fit in the vehicles. We will go to the only place we've ever been safe, which is the reservation, and hope like hell those unfortunate souls can provide some intel on their captors," Wade said.

Once Angel got through starting the fire with some of her kitchen grease and other flammables, she called 911 and wrapped her mouth with her sleeve to disguise her voice, explaining it was due to smoke. She said her bit, announced she felt woozy, and tossed her burner phone into the fire. Jake was careful to take side roads and made certain the "never to be used" pistols were in each vehicle. Eyes in the Jeep darted around every corner. The El Camino that had been left to them by a deceased former client had Ray at the wheel and kept the girls under a tarp in the back. For all their relief in escaping in the moment, ominous clouds beckoned, storming toward their immediate future. Suzette was keeping close tabs on the internet and found a news story about the fire not fifteen minutes after they left.

"Guys, it's The Pitt; the people on the news are saying not one, but two factories are ablaze on our street. They are saying it got out of control and warning onlookers to stay away, citing that the factories have barrels of crude oil and there have been two explosions already," Suzette said.

"What oil?" Deneige asked.

"The kind they brought with them to torch our place," Angel said.

In the Jeep ahead, Stan watched the rear as the specifically targeted dark roads had tall trees on either side.

"Are you sure we didn't pick up a tail? These guys aren't the cops; they aren't going to care about any land claim settlements or jurisdictions," Wade said.

"As far as a tail goes, I'm sure, but if we're about to walk into a trap and something blows up between our tires, and we bounce right into their scope range, there's no telling," Jake said.

CHAPTER 14

ANONYMOUS OBITUARIES

They drove throughout the night until reflected sunlight glistened off the dew in the grass, and serenity hummed along the sand, rocks, and water on the reservation, and all seemed tranquil. They took turns sleeping in various areas offered to them, but Stan stayed with the vehicles and kept his sidearm loaded in his belt. As morning stretched its arms toward noon, Wade found Mrs. Moran and inquired about the cult slaves.

"They want to stick together. They've been through a lot and aren't willing to separate," she said.

"Where will they stay?" Wade asked.

"I told them I could put them up for a while until we can find them a better situation, and they'd have to work. They were only too happy to, so I gave them food—careful not to overfeed them—but some of them still got sick after eating. I gave them healing roots, a lot of soups, and such, until their systems got used to eating again. They seem to be on the mend," she said.

"I need to talk to them," Wade said.

"Go ahead; they're in the field or in the lodge over there. They told me what you did for them—you and your crazy friends. The creator smiles on you," she said.

"Miigwech; I've kinda been on the short end of smiles lately," he said sheepishly.

"You're welcome. Talk to Vikki; we call her Waabaa Ajitamo; White Squirrel, she remembers her name and talks the most," she said, returning to her cooking tent.

A girl of about seventeen walked up to him, moving in a lot of different ways, almost like part of her body was walking, but other parts were shuffling in different directions as if there were some unheard music in the distance. This was undoubtedly where the squirrel reference came from. She looked prettier and less troglodyte-like now that her eyes had regained some of their lost sparkle. Despite her washed hair, clean skin, being dressed in proper clothes, and seeming less traumatized, the lingering signs of neglect still rattled him.

"Oh, hey, you're the Waiter, right?" Vikki said.

"Waiter?" he asked, confused.

"When I went to thank Stan, he told me it was all the Waiter's doing, so, like, you're a waiter, like, in a restaurant?" she asked.

"No, it's just a nickname," Wade said.

"Your name is Nick, then? I don't understand."

"No, my name is Wade. It's like if I called you 'Vik' for short; that would be a nickname, but Stan made it longer because he's, um... special! Yes, very special. That's what he is," Wade said.

"Oh, well, people think you and Ray are pretty special too for getting us out of that house, and if you wanna call me Vik to make it easier, that's okay too. Vik's the new nickname, like 'Vik the Nick'! Haha," she said.

"Vikki, I have to ask you something very important; it's delicate, but urgent. Can you help me?"

"Oh, sure, I mean, you helped us, right?"

"When I discovered you and your friends, you all mistook me for a Keeper. I need to know anything you can tell me about the Keepers. Where they go, what they do, when they come around, when they go—anything at all. Can you do that?" Wade asked.

"Oh, sure, I remember. I'm the one that bit you; I think it was on the arm," Vikki said.

"Yes, it was, and you have terrific jaw strengh and very strong teeth," Wade acknowledged.

"Oh, haha, I'm sorry! I didn't mean to bite you; I mean, I did, but I wouldn't have if I'd known you, or known it was you, or why were you there, or anything like that. I'm very sorry—quite sorry, in fact," she said.

"It's all understood and completely forgiven. Let's get back to the Keepers," Wade said.

"Oh, I don't like them very much at all. They're really mean; they'd offer us toys and then throw them in the pit to see if we'd go down and get them. They throw food too, and everyone knows not to go down there, but when you're hungry, you do crazy things," she said.

"If I saw one of them on the street, how would I know them? Do they walk or talk in a certain way? Did you ever see any scars, or a tattoo in an odd place maybe—beards, glasses, anything?" Wade asked.

"What's a tatoon? We don't know stuff because we were inside all the time," Vikki said.

"It's like a stamp on the skin, or like a picture or drawing, usually done in green ink, and it doesn't come off. Ever seen one on a Keeper?" Wade asked.

"They wore masks, but when it's hot, sometimes they take them off in their change room if no one else is around. I don't really remember what they looked like, though; it was a while ago. Try to think of better things, right? I'd do rhymes in my head. 'Keeper beeper, quit the pit,' or 'bite the bit but not in the pit,' 'see in the dark like a walk through the park.' Do you know any rhymes?" she said.

"That's fine. Those are creative, and you are doing great. I know these aren't fun questions, but if I gave you a piece of paper, could you draw one of those masks? It doesn't have to be perfect at all," Wade asked.

Vikki attempted to draw the masks, but with no art training and after having been in the dark for years, the images were indiscernible.

"I guess I'm not a very good drawer; I'm really sorry," she said with a shrug.

"It was a good try. Drawing is like a lot of things; if you practice, you can get really good no matter where you start out," Wade said, realizing he was getting nowhere.

"There is one thing I can draw for you, though," she said, as her face lit up with enthusiasm.

"What's that?" Wade said, trying to hide his disappointment.

"That thing you told me about—the tattoon! I saw one of the Keepers had it on his neck, and it was a two-headed snake going through a dollar bill. Well, not a real dollar bill, but you know how to show money with an 'S' with two lines through it; this was the same, only it was a snake with two heads going through it. Here, I'll draw it for you!" she said exuberantly.

"That's okay, Vikki! You won't have to! I know just what you mean, and I want to thank you for all the help you've given me today! You've been fantastic! Don't feel bad about the bite; it barely even left a mark, and remember, you can learn anything they can teach! You are a sharp girl, a very special young lady who will go on to great things, and don't ever let anyone tell you differently. It's been a privilege to sit here and talk with you, but I have got to run. Thank you again! Can you point me in the direction of the guy with the broken fingers? I want to apologize to him," Wade said.

"Sure, he's over there by the tent. He goes by Cody now, and thanks for talking to me," Vikki said.

"People should be thanking you! You have a great personality, and people are going to take to you like icing to cake. Just you wait and see; I'm very confident about that," he said.

"Bye, then, I guess," Vikki said.

"Hey, Cody!" Wade called out to a dark-haired youth of about seventeen.

"Oh yeah, hey," he said.

"I've been wanting to apologize to you about what happened with the fight in the dark. You didn't deserve that, and it was one hundred percent my fault. I'm sorry, and then some," Wade said.

"Yeah, well, you got us out, so I guess I can't complain too much, right?" Cody said.

"Yeah, I've been kind of all twisted up over it, and I got you something of an apology gift—not that it makes up for anything, just a token to say I know how badly I screwed up," Wade said.

"Are you gonna take it away after?" Cody asked.

"No, Cody, absolutely not! This is yours forever if you want it. You have my word! The ownership is yours, and it's permanent. It's a wristwatch, and it glows in the dark if you press this button, so you can always tell what time it is, no matter where you go. It has a beam of light that you can point at things if you ever get lost. It means you will never be stuck in darkness again. It has a locking clasp in case you are doing physical activities; it's waterproof and good for three hundred feet underwater. It's a stopwatch, shatterproof, shockproof, and a bunch of other stuff. I guess I've been thinking about time lately: how much we all might have left in the world, and how I can't go back in time and undo what I've done to you. I can't undo mistakes or fix your fingers, but I want you to know I think about it constantly," Wade said.

"For keeps, then?"

"For keeps," Wade said.

"Wow! That's awright! I wasn't really mad at you or anything, and I was trying to get you too, but this is something else; I don't think I deserve it," Cody said.

"Yes, Cody, you do. You're a very good person, and I'm ashamed of what I've done. It's my honor that you even agreed to speak to me after what happened. I'm grateful to have met you, and if you ever need a favor of any kind, I'll be there for you as long as I live, I promise," Wade said.

"You sound like you are going away; I was thinking we could be friends, maybe," Cody said.

"Sure, we can be friends, Cody, but I have to explain something to you first. Those people you call the Keepers, well, I am going to pay them a little visit and give them a piece of my mind. It's going to be pretty risky, so until I'm finished with that, I can't drag anyone into danger with me, especially someone I've already caused problems for. If I come out with all my skin intact, I'll always be your friend," Wade said.

"How can you give them a piece of your mind? You mean, like, in the chair?" Cody asked.

"No, I mean it might be time for the Keepers to be disbanded— more like that," Wade said.

"I wouldn't try it, but maybe you can. Not me, that's for sure," Cody said.

"How do I find that chair?"

"It's easy. You just go down into the pit and wander 'til you find the square hole and fall down it. They throw toys or pets down to get people to jump in, and there's no way up, so a Keeper might push you down the square hole. The hole opens up to a really big room with a long hallway. There's a shower room down there with a big hose they use on you. Then they take you down the hall to the chair, but nobody ever wants to go anywhere near there," Cody said.

"So I can get to it from inside the mansion, you're sure?" Wade asked.

"Yeah," Cody said, nodding.

"Okay, thanks, and once again, I'm terribly sorry about your hand," Wade said.

"So maybe we can hang out sometime, yeah?" Cody asked.

"Maybe we can, but I have to be clear about something, and you can tell your friend Vikki this too. I like you both very much as people, but I am in a rough line of business, and sometimes it gets messy. You and everyone who came from the manor are good people, but you've already been through enough nonsense. You see my friend Stan? He's nice, right? But doesn't he look like he could mess up a whole bunch of people if he wanted to?" Wade asked.

"Yup, he sure does."

"Okay, most of my friends are like him, so we can fight off people like the Keepers. We don't like them, and we want to see them pay for what they did to you—all of you. If we pal around with you too much, they might go after you to get back at us. It's better they don't know, and we can catch up once all our business is taken care of. One more thing: I mean what I am saying. This is not some left-handed way of avoiding being your friend. It just has to wait, understand?" Wade said.

"Oh, yeah, I get it. You got some tricky stuff to do for now, and you don't have to worry about me. I'm right-handed, and I think Vikki prolly is too, so we'll be okay with it if'n you don't like being around the lefties."

"I'm fine with lefties, I meant... well nevermind," Wade said.

Cody reached out with his healthy right hand and shook Wade's, exposing a deep red shackle mark on his wrist. Wade saw it and turned his head away before giving Cody a pat on his opposite shoulder and left.

Wade and Ray went down to a very large Army surplus store and found it bustling with activity. There were six staff members working the tills and two management types walking the floors. There were about forty people pulling at naval uniforms, WW2 relics, holsters, combat boots, and other various accoutrements. Wade noticed the sign that read, "Government employees get fifteen percent off." A stout man from India approached him and stopped for a face-to-face conversation.

"You're government security, right?" the man said, with slightly widened eyes.

Wade didn't want to be singled out for any reason, and the idea that Army veterans hunting him would have no trouble locating an army surplus store went off in his head like an alarm bell.

Wade stared at the man and said, "No-o-oh!"

The man looked down at his associate and shouted, "Anil! Let this man go downstairs. I think he's part of the government!"

There was a section curtained off by a long sheet of black vinyl with a wide set of squarely shaped stairs that changed direction three times. Wade couldn't see beyond the third set.

"Yes, okay, my friend, come down!" a voice with an Indian accent called upward.

The Indian angle didn't fit with East European soldiers, so Wade ventured down the steps, wondering what he might discover. This had always been his great flaw, and he couldn't help but wonder if the most banal and common aphorism about curiosity and a cat might script his epitaph.

"Namaste," Wade said, adjoining his palms.

"Yes, come, my friend, we have lots down here, not for regular customers," a young, fit man with a developing beard and beaming smile said, revealing a genuine enthusiasm for his work. Wade looked around, and there was a whole extra floor of goods for him to peruse. It wasn't a set-up; it might have been a case of mistaken identity, or he may have been sized up incorrectly due to his height, build, and eye color. The other possibility was that they had a policy where this was something they did to every twentieth customer or so, to make them feel cool and special. It was a wise business practice, if so, because it worked. Wade felt like he was a privileged ally of these Indian businessmen and felt included by accessing the vault others couldn't see, even if its items were all to be sold later anyhow.

He picked up a large duffle bag, camouflaged uniforms complete with helmets, holsters, boots, canteens, black-bladed boot knives, aviator glasses, face paint, three rubber gas masks, and utility belts.

If the Indian businessmen had taken him for someone in authority before, they seemed even more certain of it now, given his chosen items, and quietly gave Wade a twenty percent discount.

"What's all that?" Ray asked, looking baffled as Wade unloaded his bounty.

"Your turtle shell."

Wade took out a helmet from his bag and placed it on Ray's head.

"It's your turtle armor. I'm not sure you've built up enough emotional grit yet," Wade said, grinning.

"A red cape for the bulls?" Ray asked.

"Not for shootouts; they're disguises. I have an idea, and I want you to get Jake to paint a peel-away cover for the Jeep, all camouflage style. Tell him it's got to be a super clean job and authentic looking," Wade said.

"Of course, I'm sure he'll be thrilled! Whatever you have in mind, I'm in, but there is one caveat: if one minor detail goes wrong, we're all dead. Now, I'm not trying to put pressure on you; I'm just saying this better be your best plan yet, because there is a huge chance we're all going to become lawn fertilizer ten miles from nowhere in unmarked graves. No one is ever going to know that we were ever here. There won't even be anyone to write or pay for our obituaries. We will become unseen, unknown, and forever forgotten. If aliens are to find our time capsules jettisoned into space a million years from now, ours will be empty. We will have left no legacy, no imprint, and will have escaped history, families, and children. We are easier to erase than chalk lines in sand. So, let's get it right, okay? I don't want to become the ghost image in someone else's photo bombing session," Ray said.

"We'll be remembered by each other," Wade said.

"In the six feet under files," Ray added.

At the new place they dubbed "The Roost," given the recent sour memories of anything resembling a pit, they decided to brainstorm. Stan contributed a set of used golf clubs and had done some homework.

"The double snake in the dollar symbol isn't a jail thing; it's more of a secret society emblem. It's from an old businessman's club that grew into a shadier outfit. There's a charity organization called the Feland Foundation that helps impoverished kids get a fast track to college. They have to show good marks and come from really desperate situations— orphans from single-parent deaths, runaways from ten different foster homes, child prostitutes, homeless kids, the real tragedies. The touching part is that while getting all kinds of tax breaks for his other successful businesses, he puts a few kids through college for the tax credits. He gets a ton of applicants who are so desperate for the pot of gold at the end of the rainbow, or even a free sandwich, that they'll stand on their heads to get in his good books. These kids get interviewed and are told they didn't quite make the cut, but are then introduced to someone who might be able to help them out along the way if they can follow instructions. That's where Craven comes in. He shoots the kids a few bucks and determines whether they are watched closely or not, and suddenly he has a goldmine of kids to abuse. They'd jump for a great place to live and aren't leaving much behind. Then, the big surprise is a big mansion full of toys that hides terrible secrets inside. The symbol of the snakes had the credo of 'Seek out money, but watch where it goes after you get it.' It might have been a coy dig at petty criminals and lousy businessmen who get a big score and then blow it. Now it means, 'We've got this shady cash cow, and we'll get anyone who tries to take it.' See, they're progressive! A few years after that, many of the top dogs started wearing these devil rings with a weird geometric shape; the motto might have been, 'We are like satanists with their pentagrams, only more crooked,'" Stan said.

"How did you learn all this?" Ray asked.

"I found a guy they screwed over, and I also found out that the building by the mansion is the Feland Foundation HQ. They had that mansion declared a historical monument, so it can't be torn down, and the authorities never go near it. The headquarters has a ton of cameras and security, so any ideas about going through the front gates or climbing a fence are out," Stan said.

"I was able to get some wrist mikes and earpieces made at an electronics store because Wade hates cellphones. They're tiny, too! None of that talking into your thumb nonsense; these clip to your watch and go right inside the ear with a hollow rubber valve, all cozy and comfortable. Try 'em! Oh, and Wade, I got in touch with Mrs. Macharest.

Vikki is going to go stay with her. She'll have your old job and free tutoring to boot. Vikki left this medallion for you; it's just a random, but very unique shape. She said she hung on to it most whenever she felt she was losing her identity in the dark. It helped her stay focused and always be true to herself. I told her you didn't believe in anything spiritual, and she said you could think of it as an atheist's cross if you like. Now that she's free, she doubts she'll need it anymore and wants you to have it. Cody loves the watch you got him, and now all we have to do is hear your plan to make sure we all aren't a bunch of anonymous corpses within a day or two," Suzette said, exuding a facetious, joyful grin.

"I don't care what happens to us; I want to get my hands on the subhuman assholes who messed up those people. Some of them were just kids," Jake said with cold fury in his eyes.

"Take it easy there, Agamemnon. We don't need our asses getting shot because we're acting ten feet tall," Angel said.

"Those scumbags are abominations, and I'm going to make 'em pay the ticket price for making a place like that," Jake said sternly.

"Can we hear what Wade has to say before you go running out of here, all trigger-happy?" Angel asked.

"Jake's not wrong for wanting his pound of flesh, but we are going to be careful. If our timing is off by even a single breath, we might all be slow dancing under the daisy garden," Wade said.

"Oh, goody, I love it when we might all die because someone forgot they had to take a leak," Ray said.

"Ray, you had the toughest go last time out, so you'll be the cameraman getting license plates and calling the cops. Suzette, you'll be with him, working the phones and following suit. Jake, Stan, and I go back to the stink house with the gas masks."

"Guns?" Deneige asked.

"Only for Ray, and all he has to do is take out one windowpane and fire a few shots into the air," Wade said.

"And how does everyone stay alive, avoiding the death squad looking for us?" Suzette asked.

"We're going to the one place they won't expect us: the darkest, smelliest mansion in the world. Does anyone think you can hire a pricey foreign militia group to camp out at Stench Manor for days at a time? We won't know where they are, but it won't be there," Wade said.

"Ray, you'll wait half a mile ahead of the foundation's admin office with your earpiece ready. Now, lady and gents, we go!"

"What do I do?" Angel asked indignantly.

"You stay here and keep Deneige safe. Maybe you can make a phone call for me, and Angel, if you cook something, try not to start a fire," he said.

Jake drove the El Camino with its tail end right up to the repaired doors to the mansion. He hooked up a cable and winch to lower them into the second pit. Jake took out a crowbar, Stan took out the aluminum bats, and Wade grabbed the high-powered flashlights. They wore tight turtlenecks and jogging tights under their military uniforms in case they had to run fast. Once inside, they went straight into the pit to locate tunnels. The beams of the flashlights only added to the sense of foreboding and repellent nature of the former estate. From within the gas masks, the glowing beams mixed with the dank atmosphere, creating various greenish hues for most of what they saw. The pit was essentially an uprooted basement with housed bones, burnt ashes, packaged toys, and bits of used gauze and surgical tape carelessly strewn about.

The floor was uneven—hard and flat in some areas and a mixture of hardwood, earth, and soil in others. Stan nearly lost his balance at the footing of a square opening that must have been an old cellar missing its trap door. Stan jumped across and pulled himself up over a twelve-foot drop to the lower floor.

"This must be it!" he said.

Jake grabbed the cable, hooked it to his belt, and jumped down. Stan collected the slack and jumped next. Wade told them they were both rushing too much and that they had to monitor the time very closely.

As they observed their surroundings, they noticed a dangling metal lamp with a pull cord and a single bulb, and Stan shook his head in case anyone thought to use it. Just beyond that, they noticed an open shower area with no stalls or benches but a thick hose that was housed into the bottom of a wall.

There were two corridors to follow, and Stan took one on the condition he return in two minutes, while Jake and Wade followed the other.

As they neared the corridor's end, they saw a thick door and switched off their lights.

"This is an unforeseen problem—most likely a skeleton crew of a few guys on standby. When Stan gets back, we spring the door and go to town with the bats; we don't have time to do it any other way," Wade whispered.

"Where the flying hell is Stan?" Jake whispered back.

The high-powered beam came shooting across the door from behind them as both Jake and Wade simultaneously waved their fingers in front of their necks from side to side, energetically signaling for Stan to turn off his light. Once he did, the suffocating darkness drowned out all remnants of shape and contour. They could not see the door. Jake put his ear to the wall where he thought the door had been, while Stan put his ear to the floor. He heard the muffled sound of another door being shut in the background and voices. Wade felt for and found the door handle. Then he grabbed the arm of each man and slowly tapped it once, then twice, then placed his bat in their palm. Then he started again—once, twice—and then he ripped open the door and lunged into the room. It was a locker room, and there were two men smoking marijuana, while a third was on his phone. A guard with long sideburns looked up at the three bat-wielding door crashers, dropped his phone, grabbed an electronic cattle prod, and instantly thrust it into Jake's stomach.

There was a quick and quiet momentary hum as Jake dropped to the floor with a heavy grunt. Wade swung his bat over Jake's fallen body and cracked the guard with the cattle prod across the side of the head with full force. The man's head tilted to his shoulder, and it snapped out of position as he fell to the floor. Both of the blunt smokers grabbed cattle prods as well, but Stan dropped his bat in favor of hand-to-hand combat. He grabbed a long-haired man by the forearm and twisted it toward his assailant until he dropped his weapon. Wade then cracked the long-haired man over the head and hit him twice more on the side of the head before he could react. The third man turned to run, but Stan jumped on his back and pulled him to the ground before he reached the door. Wade tossed him a bat, and Stan used it to put his opponent into a chokehold, and he quickly rendered him unconscious.

Jake got up in an astonishing fury, and as the guard who'd stuck him with the prod was coming to and rubbing his forehead, which had already had a fist-sized, hematoma rapidly growing out of it.

"You wanna zap me like a fuckin' cow?" Jake screamed.

He clutched the cattle prod and zapped the Keeper over and over, who replied only in abrupt exhortations of pain.

"Here! How do *you* like it?"

bzzzzt. "Unghhhh!"

"You hit fuckin' kids with this?"

bzzzzt. "AGH!"

"Here!"

bzzzzzt. "Aghhhhhhh!"

The security man with the long sideburns fell to the ground, making pathetic whimpering sounds as Jake struck him with the prod right beside his swelling hematoma before tossing it aside. Stan turned toward the door, but their friend was still enraged. He picked up the aluminum bat, and Wade had to grab him as Stan pulled the bat out of Jake's trembling hands.

"I'll fuckin' kill him!" Jake said, wild-eyed.

Stan placed the perverse guard in a chokehold, with the man's shoulder cutting off his blood supply from his neck, and he quickly passed out.

"Jake, how many times have you hated it when we had to keep Stan from going out of control? Right now, he's helping me do that with you. Think about that! We don't have time for this, and we have to be a million times more silent than you are being right now," Wade whispered, pointing at his watch.

Jake slowly nodded as he was nothing if not a team player, but he was so livid that no one was sure what he might do next. Stan opened the door, and Wade signaled Jake for silence as they ventured forward. Fortunately, the corridor was long enough that they may not have been heard, but there was no way to know. After a long walk, they came to a well-lit room with a single chair in it and floodlights overhead. There was an adjoining room hidden behind it that served as a side station for cleanup. There was bleach to clean blood and destroy DNA evidence, and there were bandages, alcohol, and some unsavory metal instruments for inducing pain.

Jake's head reeled in disgust as Wade's eyes tightened, holding back his own anger.

"Maybe we should bring a few of these for the bosses," Stan said.

"We have to stay cool; on the other side of that hallway, we'll be on camera. Masks on, and bats only!" Wade said.

Wade opened the door, and opposite them was a security guard in a black uniform with a .45 automatic pointed at them.

"Drop the bats, or I'll drop you! Up against the wall! Now!" He shouted.

"We're the hired help," Stan said.

"Shut up, and take those masks off. Slow-ow-ly," the unwavering guard said.

"Aren't you supposed to call someone first to verify that?" Jake said.

"I said, shut up! You'd know who's in charge instead of saying 'someone,' asshole, if you were the hired help."

"You mean like Mr. Craven," Wade said, guessing.

"You know Craven?" the stern guard with intense, alert brown eyes said.

"Cool tattoo! I've got the same one," Stan said, noticing the double snake symbol on his neck.

"Shut the hell up right now or get popped; I was talking to him," the guard said, pointing his gun at Wade.

"I can't get it off," Wade said, tugging at his mask.

"Against the wall!"

Stan and Jake turned their backs to the guard and faced the wall as instructed, still reluctant to remove their masks until they were forced to. Still, with the camouflaged face paint they wore, revealing their faces was moot. Wade bent down, pulling off his mask, and swung his body upward, swinging the gas mask at the gun. Jake lunged toward the guard and got him in a body lock, and the three swung around in a struggle for the gun. Just as they were about to topple, Stan put everything he had into his batter's swing as the sound of aluminum striking bone rang out, making a loud clunk that echoed, and the guard fell on his back, staring blankly with his hands outstretched above him for five seconds before they fell by his side.

"Get his gun!" Stan said, pulling the guard's cellphone and calling Suzette.

Wade was about to hand it to Jake, but he put it on his belt instead.

"This guy's not legit security," Stan said.

"And I know where he got his uniform," Wade added.

"Suzette, when you hear the line go through, go for it!" Stan said, after reaching the last number called.

Craven, a brown-haired man with a mustache and strong physique, was transferring funds on his laptop.

"Craven! You're screwed! Those kids causing all the problems are dead, but Feland doesn't trust you anymore, and he sent the mercs to kill you, too," she said and hung up.

Just then, Ray fired the target rifle into Craven's office from just outside of camera range. One small portion of the windowpane broke as shards rained down, shattering into smaller pieces, and Craven moved away from the window. The door flew open, and Craven leaped out of the way in an attempt to reach his desk drawer.

"Looking for one of these?" Wade said, waving the .45 at him.

"What are you doing? Why? This makes no sense!" Craven insisted.

"Tell Feland we're here and we didn't get paid in full yet, and we're going to kill him too if he doesn't get down here, like yesterday," Wade said.

Craven hesitated, so Jake walloped him across the knees with a bat, which made him yelp like a dog and grimace as he rocked forward, sucking in air before he nodded.

"Mr. Feland! It's the team you hired. They've gone nuts! They killed those kids, and now they want more money. They shot at me, and they're coming for both of us unless you show up here with more cash," Craven said into the phone.

"Nonsense! This is preposterous! They've been well compensated and readily agreed to terms. This doesn't fit at all; I'm afraid I'm not inclined to believe you," Feland said.

"Well, they shot up the foundation windows, dragged a bat across my knees, and shoved a .45 in my face. Do you believe me now?" Craven shouted.

"A bat!? Not likely! Indeed, stay there, Craven, stall them as best you can. Help is on the way," Feland said and hung up.

"Good boy!" Wade said.

Stan was examining the desk for a weapon as Jake opened whatever cabinets he could find. He found a medieval henchman outfit, a mask, and a high-powered cattle prod neatly folded and charged.

"Now what?" Craven demanded.

"I think we just found our chair host, the chairman of the board, you might say, right, Craven?" Jake asked in a calm and almost soothingly relaxed tone.

"That's not mine!" Craven roared.

"Did you know a kid got broken fingers because we thought he was one of you?" Jake asked in the same cool, collected tone.

Nearly two miles away, a black SUV carrying military personnel had its license plate photographed by a zoom lens as a target rifle fired several shots into the air and then came roaring out of the bushes. Suzette called the police non-emergency line while Ray stepped on the gas.

"Hello, Police! My name is Sheryl Rooney, and I'm out on East 49 side road off of old Highway 16, and there is this black SUV swerving all over the road, and they're firing guns and tossing beer cans out of the windows. It's a custom license plate. It definitely looks like a drunken driver with his yahoo buddies. Oh, my cell is dying, I just wanted to—" she said and hung up.

Ray took out a burner phone and dialed 911.

"Hey, you guys better get out here right away; there's a drunk driver in the wrong lane who just nearly drove into me, and I was barely able to get away. If that's not enough, the guys in there were waving firearms around laughing their heads off, like it was funny. Very dangerous! Custom plates! East 49 off Highway 16: Send somebody out now!"

The SUV stopped and turned toward them before turning again and heading back toward the Feland Foundation. Once safely out of view, Ray pulled over and removed the camouflaged magnets Jake provided to disguise the Jeep as they tossed burner phones and magnets into a garbage bag and disposed of them at the next rest stop.

"Let's see these guys explain a car full of weapons on U.S. soil and their fatigues after ten at night to local cops. That Browning ain't exactly for skeet shooting, haha!" Ray said, grinning.

At the Feland Foundation, Jake had run out of questions for Craven. He picked up the dungeon master's uniform and threw it at Craven.

"You know I can't let you ever touch that cattle prod again. You must *know* that," Jake said.

"It's not mine, I told you!" Craven said.

"If true, I'd think you'd want to try it on and prove it doesn't fit," Jake said.

Craven turned his head away, and Jake told him he could reach for the gun in the desk, and Craven jumped at the chance, but Jake kicked the drawer shut on his fingers. Then he pretended to open it and slammed them again, crushing several digits as Craven screamed.

"Is that how it sounded when you put kids and women in that chair for the guests?" Jake asked.

Craven dove across the floor, reaching for the cattle prod, and Jake stepped on the fingers of his other hand and stood tall on them, applying his weight on the hand with the same black ring Feland wore, as Craven shouted derogatory epithets about Natives.

"See? That's why you should never wear gaudy jewelry!" Jake said.

"Okay, that's enough, Jake! This all hinges on timing. Get him out of his clothes and paint his face," Wade instructed.

Stan provided his military uniform for Craven to change into, while Jake painted Craven's face in camouflaged greasepaint.

"You can't do this! They're going to think I'm one of you!" Craven howled.

"What's wrong with that? You don't have any qualms about sending precision assault teams after people, do you?" Wade asked.

"Fuck! They're here already!" Jake said as he picked up the .45 and fired some warning shots toward the SUV from the broken window.

"That's our cue!" Wade called out.

"Wait! That other tunnel I ran down leads to a weird graveyard; we can get out through it unseen," Stan said urgently.

"Grab his keys, lock him in here, and let's jet!" Wade said.

After locking all the doors and grabbing their bats, the three ran full speed back through the corridors they entered. With no time to strip down, they passed the chair and found Stan's alternate route out. They exited what looked to be an odd temple, with uninviting, jagged shapes protruding from all its edges. There were recent graves with old tombstones from an era long since gone, and many of them had chalk names written over the old names. Jake wondered aloud if the freed victims corrected some of the ones they knew, but Wade wasn't answering as something caught his eye. On an arc-shaped slab of stone that read "Abigail Daeva (1840–1907)," the word "Melanie" was written across it in chalk, with childlike handwriting. Gradually, the sounds of sirens grew in the distance.

"C'mon, Wade, it's probably just a coincidence," Jake said.

"I can see the side of the mansion from here, and I saw an old, damaged welcome sign inside that read 'Balcom Manor' on it," Stan said.

"Like the fixer! We'd better get to the car," Jake said.

Wade and Jake removed their fatigues, put them in a bag with the gas masks, and drove past the Foundation headquarters to see the police detaining the mercenaries and confiscating weapons from their SUV.

CHAPTER 15

A SKEWED CALLING

Back at The Roost, Deneige and Angel were having a heart-to-heart conversation about the future.

"So, do you think you'll ever get married?" Angel asked.

"To Wade, you mean? Oh, I don't know. He's so unbounded by anything, he answers to no one, and he's almost without vices to help him through. There's almost nothing there for a girl to get her hooks into, as the men say," she said, smiling.

"Yeah, but he's very good with kids. I've seen him," Angel said.

"Sure, but we're not like you and Jake; you'll soon be engaged, and then babies, and all that fun stuff. Now you are someone a person could bank on; you'll be a vessel for a young life, and you'll care for it all your years. See, that's a life worth... well, a responsible person with something to live for," Deneige said.

"Right, but Jake didn't exactly arrive wanting to start a family; I had to work on him for a while first. The good ones are always worth putting the time into."

"Oh, for sure, it's just that I have antiquated ideas about soul mates, forevermore, and all that. I just want to be sure that I'm hitching my wagon to someone ready for the long haul. While I'm absolutely interested in keeping him around, I wonder if he'd ever want to be a kept man, so to speak," Deneige said.

"They all want to be kept, cooked for, and taken care of when they are sick. Deep down, they are all looking for a second-hand mother with fringe benefits," Angel said.

"I am so not up to date on these things. I thank you for your sage advice, but I need to check something at home. I'll just be a few hours, just to the house and back, okay?" Deneige asked.

"I'm not your master; you go ahead and live your life. It's just usually when we promise the guys to stay put when they're on a mission for safety reasons that we do it, but you're a free woman; there are no chains on you here," Angel said.

"Thanks for understanding, and I'll bring you some macaroons. Jake's lucky to have you," Deneige said.

A few minutes before midnight, all were back at The Roost, unloading stress from all directions.

"Hey! A full head count, and everyone is still breathing," Stan said, raising his glass.

"Yeah, we're all still alive, but that was getting past the point of just being dicey. I think I'm going to pack it in, boys. Angel and I want to get married and raise a couple of kids. I saw a side of myself I didn't like very much tonight. I got past the point of keeping my humanity intact, and I wanted to kill so badly that I was just about drooling to do it. That's not the guy I want raising my kids, and seeing the inside of that place changes you. It changes the honest answers you can give your kids when they ask questions. I hate to say it, guys, but I'm out. Sorry!" Jake said.

"You don't owe anybody anything," Stan said.

"We talked it over, and while we love you guys, we just don't see much future in this kind of work," Angel added.

"What will you do for work?" Ray asked.

"I'll probably go back to racing and fixing cars. When you think about our money, which was good but split six or seven ways, and all the surveillance equipment, weapons, and other equipment, it goes fast. We were turning into a paramilitary operation, and I, for one, never wanted to join the army," Jake said.

"Maybe we should get married," Ray said, half joking, but looking directly at Suzette.

"Maybe, it's not a bad idea; looking at me swinging a rolling pin is far safer than dodging snipers," Suzette said.

"Congratulations to the four of you! I'll be the first to admit this one went miles beyond the norm, and we're lucky to be here to talk it out. I can't thank all of you enough for the risks, the finesse, and the teamwork everyone in this group has provided since we started," Wade said.

"...and then there were two," Stan said.

"What about you, Stan? Surely we can't do this on our own without digging our own graves. What will you do next?" Wade asked.

"I'll take my share of the money, and get a big motorcycle, quit regular life, and ride the highways. I'm going to check out the other side of the horizon. I've always wanted to do that," he said.

"I don't want to break up the after party, but I've been checking the news, and Craven is dead. He had his throat cut. Those military guys sure work quick! That could have been us if they'd had a few more seconds," Suzette said.

"Wouldn't they just shoot him?" Ray asked.

"The cops were on them right after they got there; it doesn't fit," Stan said.

"Maybe one of them ran up some stairs and gutted a fish. Maybe the guy who wears the suit, and makes the calls," Deneige said.

"Maybe he got away, and he is looking for payback too," Wade said.

Angel scurried to the window, and Riley followed her, running from window to window.

"Wait a second! There is this website that follows cops around to make sure they aren't violating people's constitutional rights, and they get all kinds of classified information. They are saying Craven was part of a ritual killing. That doesn't sound very much like mercenary work to me," Suzette said.

"It has to be Feland. He's the only missing link left," Stan said.

"I thought he'd be rattled enough to run for it. Maybe Feland is a little tougher than we thought. He's not the only one on the list we should be keeping an eye on. What happens when those soldiers of fortune pay their fines or whatever, thinking we pinned a murder on them? Hell, they might even think we did it! They could be telling the cops that right now," Jake said.

"It sure would suck if we all went out separate ways, and they came after us one by one. Imagine if we're busy with our guards down, trying out the good life," Stan said.

"Explaining our whereabouts to the cops doesn't sound very sexy either, especially if they've been fed a bunch of bullshit first," Ray added.

"Look at where this life has taken you, Wade. I can appreciate an adrenaline rush like anyone else, but this business of having your lives on the line with every new wrinkle in every plan, there is always some detail no one could have predicted, pointing to you all dying for naught. Listen to your friends; they want to get on with their lives so they can have meaning, have families, and have futures. We don't have to get married tomorrow or even talk about that, but let's go somewhere and have peace in our lives. It could be a cabin, some sleepy little town, or up in the mountains. We could have all that if we dropped this obsession of yours and just led normal lives. Can't you see that?" Deneige asked.

"I met her," Wade said.

"What?" Deneige asked.

"Your sister! Some of her creepy buddies were trying to kill her when I was a little kid. She killed two or three of them, and I got the worst one, the leader. I was around twelve. That's how I knew it couldn't be her body; she made it clear for me to get away and crawled off on some rock, saying she needed a nap. I was so dumb, I believed her. She saved my life, and I left her behind, probably hiding a gunshot wound to her stomach. Nobody tortured her; nobody broke her ankles. She found the most comfortable place she could, and waited for death to meet her across the river," Wade said.

"All this time, and you never said one word about it?" Deneige asked.

"Well, he can't exactly print that on a T-shirt, now, can he?" Stan asked, sounding irritated.

"I guess I should have left the whole thing alone, and now we're all in a jam," Wade said.

"No, I think I can understand. She was probably trying to recruit you, those people, and their kind; that's what they do: recruit kids. They get them in a bad situation, then become the only hand ready to help. Next, they draw you in, ever deeper into the abyss. They'll use anything: food, emotional support, sex appeal, whatever it takes," Deneige said.

"What about Feland?" Angel asked.

"If he got to Craven, he's definitely got people out looking for us," Ray said.

"We won't give him the chance. Jake and Angel can go to the reservation; no one will look there. Ray and Suzette can rent horses and go through the trails to Mrs. Moran's, and boat across the water to Fallen Star point. Take just enough for camping, and don't tell anyone where you are going. Stan can get a helmet with a smoked visor and disappear on the highways," Wade said.

"What about you, and Deneige?" Angel asked.

"She'll be safe at home. No one knows she has any involvement in this," Wade said.

"And you?" Jake asked.

"I'll lay low for a bit, and if Feland tries to make his presence felt, I know where he lives. If not, I'll follow suit and try to build a life with Deneige, if she'll have me," Wade said.

"You sure you're not going to push this?" Stan asked.

"And what about Feland? He gets a pass to just dream up some plan to seek us out for years, does he?" Jake asked.

"As of this moment, our little troupe is no longer. If he comes for me, it'll be one-on-one, and I'm okay with that. If the mercenaries don't get their legal expenses covered, they'll be pissed and won't want to work using their own funds. They might even take issue with Feland themselves. The longer we keep swimming against the current, the more problems we run into. We've come to our senses, and so let's be smarter people from now on; besides, if she ever dumps me, I'll still have Riley," Wade said, smiling.

"I knew you'd finally come to your senses, and that makes me happy too," Deneige said.

Hugs, high fives, and handshakes were shared repeatedly, and a few sets of eyes were wiped just as often. A mixture of excitement over the future and the fears of dissolving the only semi-functional family they'd ever known stirred their emotions like eggs and ice cream in a blender. Three days went by as the disbanded surrogate family members sought to expand their horizons and find safer employment. Last good-byes were shared, and a call came from Mrs. Macharest inviting Wade and Deneige for a special dinner as Vikki had proven a remarkably quick study and had no one to show how much she'd learned. He agreed but put things off for a week and laid out his bat, flashlight, and fedora for one last trip to Balcom Manor. He'd call Feland to meet him there, and avoid being jumped by any hired goons he might meet at Feland's home. Wade called a cab and placed his bat in a garbage bag with some odds and ends to ease any stress a cabbie might experience at the point of pickup. His claimed destination was one town north of the foundation, but as they neared Balcom Manor, Wade selected a part of the road that would be a suitable distance for him to walk unnoticed.

"Oh, Blast! I forgot my damn cell phone. Never mind, here's twenty bucks. I'll just walk back from here," he said.

Once the tail lights vanished into the merging point where the road met the night sky at the horizon, he ventured toward the manor.

He didn't go to the entrance but instead approached the graveyard behind it. He stepped around old styled tombs with little markings as some stones only had first names and some only one year, which he found odd. There were a few with the names scratched out and new names in chalk like Abigail's was when the name had been changed to Melanie. He removed his bat and left the bag near the grave. Wade noticed the graves seemed shallow, about half their normal depth, which meant abnormally frequent use, or someone was digging them up for unknown reasons. He stepped into the entrance way, which consisted of a smallish metal door with pointed angular spikes on its archway. There were holes on either side for bars to barricade it, yet no bars to enact the function. He left his coat on a stone and put the garbage bag on top to hide it. The door was stiff, so he put his foot to it, then his shoulder, and it clanked and scraped as it gave way. The years of dampness did most of his work for him. Once again, he was stunned over how the unearthly darkness seemed to all but suffocate the use of one's eyes. It made him think about how within a black hole, the gravity is so dense that even light or other particle waves could not escape it. If it wasn't gravity causing this exceptional darkness, he couldn't say what was.

He pulled out his flashlight and noticed there were chalk lines and misshapen drawings that looked to have been drawn by a child. The idea struck him that coming from the darkened manor, the work might have been from an adult with hampered vision. This also meant that whoever scrawled Melanie's name across Abigail's grave may also have been an adult, but for what possible reason, he pondered.

There was a loud slamming of a metal door from the direction that he came. Wade ran at full speed down the corridor only to hear the sound of a pipe sliding into a fixture on the other side. A second slid across the door with a resounding clunk upon completion. Wade didn't wait for a third and ran back to find the chair room, which would lead to the foundation and a proper exit. He turned down the wrong passage, which led to the loathsome pit. It had been cleaned out, but the residual odor was nothing he wanted to revisit. Then he heard footsteps, those of a very large man, followed by the clink of a chain. There were only three corridors, but they looked exactly the same. Wade ran in the opposite direction from the sound, which only led him in a circle back to the pit. Wade switched off his light. He walked ten quiet paces and bent down, listening in silence. He placed his light by his knee and gripped his bat blindly in utter darkness. Gradually, the shifting weight of a large man neared him as his motion rattled a length of chain that Wade suspected was across his shoulders. He began to time the seconds between each step until he felt certain they were within two feet of each other, and Wade swung his bat for all he was worth. The low pitched sound of aluminum cutting through the air indicated he'd missed his target. He swung again at nothing and spun around to determine if this hunting predator had slipped past him and swung again to no avail. Then a hum and crackle cut through his thoughts as a jolt went through his ribs, causing him to fall forward. As he got up, another shot from the cattle prod with a lot more juice struck his ribs and sent him sprawling across the floor as he grunted. He kicked outward with his left foot and swung high with his right fist, hitting nothing, as the prod struck again just over his ear, and he hit the floor again, and didn't get up. When he came to, he found his left ankle shackled to what he thought was a post.

"You're not half the challenge expected," a low, even voice said over a loudspeaker.

"Feland! Is that you?"

A large booted foot kicked him in the stomach, and while he attempted to clutch at it, he fell backward and dangled in the square shaped hole he originally thought might have been a cellar.

"Speaking without permission is inadvisable," the voice taunted.

"So is ducking a fair fight," Wade shouted into the darkness, dangling upside down from one chained foot with blood rushing to his head. He vowed to himself that if he ever got loose, he would abandon all rules of the fighter's code and embrace every dirty trick imaginable to accommodate all of his mounting rage.

"Take off your clothes," the voice said flatly.

"What? Not a chance, creep!"

"You don't want to earn a demerit point for disobedience, do you?" the voice mocked.

"Oh, come on, let's just have a serious tilt on even ground. If you win, you get to do anything, and I'll even let you use the cattle prod for an added advantage, just don't be such a gutless coward," Wade said, straining his voice.

"You could be on even ground. You'd have a little fall to the floor below, but there's a nice shower for cleanup. You know things will get worse for you down there, but you are starting to want to be on a flat surface to stop that pounding at your temples. You'll never get a reset if you don't follow directions. How long can you stay like this? Let's see. I'll be back in five minutes, and if your clothes aren't in the shower below for cleanup, you might just be hanging around for days. Hungry, weakened, ready to give up, or even worse," the impartial, low voice announced.

Wade removed his shirt and belt, then tried to lasso the chain with the belt to prop himself up, but it kept slipping down the chain above his leg. He could barely reach one boot, folding himself upward against gravity, as he had to remove his boot knife without dropping it. He dropped the empty boot first and freed the knife, putting the handle in his mouth. As he undid the other boot, he slipped through the chain's grip and fell, clutching his arms around his head to avoid a concussion as he crashed to the ground. It hurt his back, and the only moral victory beyond a small boot knife was the fact that he'd kept his pants on.

He felt around for his boots, having concentrated on the sound as each landed. Suddenly, a glaring flood of bright light came from a wall of huge circular lights, all joined together. It was so bright that even with closed eyes, he could see a reddish imprint on his shut eyelids. Then the blast from a thick fire hose knocked him from his feet, and each time he tried to stand, it thrust him against the back wall, pinning him against it. The lights flickered rapidly, oscillating between the exposures of extreme dark to intense light. Wade knew better than to open his eyes, as the goal was to damage his vision, so the Keepers could never be identified.

"Undress, and then after some questions, you can sleep in a comfortable cell. You want a comfortable place to sleep, don't you? You don't want to keep getting washed down over and over," the voice said.

Then the next hose blast knocked him from his feet, and he heard a light piece of metal skip across ceramic tiles from the force of the water. He knew his best chance of escape had been flushed away with his knife, both forever lost to the dark.

"I'm going to keep that. Wouldn't it be ironic if you ended up getting gutted by your own tiny, little knife?" the voice asked.

Wade heard the same footsteps that eluded him earlier, and even with his eyes closed, he could tell the blinding floodlights were still on. He reasoned that his captor had to be wearing some sort of special light-reducing eyewear that quelled the retina-damaging brightness. He hoped they would at least be as large as night vision goggles so that he might pry them off, but a darker thought struck him. If that henchman had a high-powered cattle prod and Wade was soaking wet, he might die of electrocution from a single jolt. Wade's fighting IQ was always fairly high, and he needed it now. He remembered the earlier kick was to the stomach; the zap was to the ribs. The hired muscle didn't like to leave obvious marks and tended to strike above the waist. The gushing water on the floor was interrupted by sparse splashes as the henchman's steps grew nearer. Wade missed him earlier with the bat, which meant the goon had a flexible torso, so aiming at the thug's head would be pointless with eyes shut. When the boot splashing sounded about three feet away, Wade hurled himself toward the unseen legs of the burly man. Once he determined the leg position, he grabbed the man's groin with his left hand, trying to crush whatever was there. With his right, he punched furiously at the remainder of that target area as the two men tumbled down. His captor wailed in agony, and the cattle prod was heard skittering across the floor. Wade was in frenzy mode, firing a cyclone of punches and clutching recklessly at the skull of his foe. He felt some special light-altering goggles and ripped them from the brute's oversized cranium. He hurled them violently when a hard punch knocked him off balance from a muscular man who knew how to hit. Wade flew backwards as the blow tested the durability of his jaw. Then the sound of floundering in the water grew louder as his assailant began swinging wildly. The aggressor failed, however, to listen to the room's clues of position and movement. Wade wished the Adam's apple gave more sound, but he could hear his attacker's breathing, for a little air escaped each time his opponent missed a punch. Wade threw a kick to the shin that landed flush and spun his attacker a quarter turn.

Both men kept moving in little leaps to advance position, trying desperately not to slip on the watery floor.

Occasionally, Lady Luck unexpectedly arrives in a low-cut dress with an uncorked bottle of wine. Wade threw a wild haymaker based on the timing of his opponent's steps, and the sound of his fist hitting bone echoed off the walls. Wade marched his feet forward, following the sound of the henchman's retreating steps. He then connected with a left to the mouth and a walloping right to the cheekbone, hastening the retreat. Wade walked him back, punching him with every second step, as he'd miss one but the next connected. He repeated this blind attack until they crossed the full distance of the room. For the release of his last burst of rage, Wade launched an unorthodox right hook that struck the temple, and the dungeon master fell backward, splashing into the water. Wade seized his foe, looking to teach him the meaning of ground and pound. The unseen enemy grunted as he fell and was dazed but still got up, inches from Wade's guess, swinging his fists wildly and swearing.

"You're fuckin' dead!" he growled loudly.

Wade darted toward the voice, recognizing it was deeper than the one on the intercom, seeking to pinpoint from where it stemmed, then jumped on guesswork. Reaching the back of the man's neck, biting down hard on his ear, he locked it in his teeth, pushing his tormentor's skull away with both hands. The disoriented thug yelped and shrieked like an injured animal, lunging forward suddenly to break the grip. Wade now understood precisely where he was and sprang onto his back again, placing him in a chokehold. The burly henchman backed Wade into a wall with enough force to knock the wind out of him. Wade still held on, squeezing with every ounce of his strength, but they were slippery from the water, and he felt his grip loosening. Involuntarily, he opened his eyes for a moment as the piercing light seared into his brain, but among the flickering spots between reactive blinks, he saw the amulet Vicki had given him on the floor, and he knew he couldn't let go. He tightened his grip under the chin and locked it in. The dungeon master rocked and twisted violently, but that only sunk the grip in deeper. The brute flailed his arms wildly and unsuccessfully tried to say something before he collapsed into a heap. Fearing any fakery, Wade continued to squeeze until the man fell limp. He lifted an arm, and it dropped immediately, certain the sadist was out cold. He felt around for the goggles, and finally he could see. Wade walked over to the man, tempted to further disable him. He hesitated, looking down, craving serenity, a humdrum life, and inner peace. He could not believe his life decisions had landed him here in this ominous palace of torment. His tolerance was tested, he was sick of fighting, sick of unending violence, being on edge, wondering who'd seek him out, or hire someone to find him over past conflicts. It was only a matter of time, but he knew if he allowed the slightest opportunity for this monster to repeat his behavior, it would be little better than participating in heinous crimes himself. He understood the compassion he felt separated him from his opponents; he wasn't a psycho, and he'd never harm an innocent or kill anyone. What he wouldn't give however, for a moment of life spent by a cabin in the woods. Battle fatigue was setting in, but this was no time for an excuse as he understood, too, that going soft now would only aid the brooding evil that dwelled in this place. Becoming an enabler for the sadists or harming a downed opponent was an ugly choice, leaving him with no comfortable solution. Wade only fought for purpose, but after today, he'd reevaluate his principles, yet it had to wait. He grabbed the index finger on each hand and snapped them back until he heard multiple cracks as the henchman flew up from his mini coma, screeching.

"Don't worry. After a few questions, you can sleep in a nice, comfortable bed," Wade spoke mimicking the voice from the loudspeakers with the same condescending tone of cold, clinical detachment.

"You son of a bitch, when I get my hands on you, look whacha fuckin' did to me!" the henchman raged. "I'll stomp your last fuckin' breath atta ya."

Wade grabbed one of the broken fingers and tipped it back, causing his sadistic foe to twist and writhe off balance. The thickly built goon had to traipse carefully to avoid more disjointed digits as Wade twisted them to the verge of breaking and bent his wailing adversary to his will. Anger and disgust guided him to the chair without mercy when Wade strapped him in.

"There you go, big fella. That's quite the little costume, all black leather, S and M style, for gorillas with no personality or social skills, and I like the mask, but it's gotta go," Wade said.

Wade removed the mask to see a strong-looking face with a unibrow and a swollen red welt on his cheekbone.

"I was hoping for a senator or chief of police or someone more impressive. You look like a dumb, 'roid addict who never got laid. Who the hell are you?"

He didn't answer.

"After what you did to me, you can't be dumb enough to think you won't tell me. You think I'm going to feel sorry for a three-dollar-bill misfit? I don't *like* you, understand?" Wade chided as he grabbed two fingers from the man's right hand and pried them apart.

"This is for Melanie!" he said, snapping the index finger sideways 'til it cracked and lay fixed, out of place closer to the thumb.

"AAAAGGHHH! You fucking eel! They're gonna kill you in the worst ways, just wait!"

"Wrong answer!" Wade said, and jabbed the screaming henchman in the eye with his index finger hard enough that the roughneck's shouts barely drowned out the squishing sound.

"Owwww aagh! Fuck! My eye! Fuckin' hell! Okay, asshole! I'm Frank Sacco, from the Bronx," he said.

"I always liked the Bronx. I'm not sure they'll take you back when this gets out," Wade said.

"Dammit!" Frank said.

"Why is everyone in the free world wanting me dead or worse?" Wade demanded.

"Ya really gotta ask? There's a lotta people wanting to know just who in na fuck you are!"

Wade punched him hard in his Adam's apple, producing a brief cough and gurgle; then Frank took several moments to regain his voice and collected himself.

"Do you think I want games here?" Wade asked pointedly.

"Because ya wouldn't leave the damn thing alone with the dead chick! She was an FBI informant, and that got her killed right away. Some local press guys caught wind of it, and da feds had to bust a few moves to kill the story. It didn't go down so well, and people got in shit over it. Then you come around stickin' your dick in everyone's mashed potatoes, and they can't pull your file. They started callin' you The Eel because they can't run your driver's license, close your bank account, or cancel your credit cards. Nothin'! That freaks those kinda people out; then they start thinkin' maybe you work for someone, only they can't figure out who. Then they watch you, and they get even more confused. Ya gave 'em the slip a few times, don't go out much, no school records, no rap sheet, no phone. They have to justify their jobs tracin' n' trackin' people and don't much like gettin' stymied, no freakin' way. Their bosses like it a lot less."

"And how do you know all this?"

"Because I don't say shit when I'm workin'. People start to forget that I can even talk, and I become part of the woodwork."

"In your little leather jammies?"

"You stay quiet enough, they'll forget ya, dressed as the Statue of Liberty," Frank said.

"Melanie was an informant?"

"Damn straight she was. They was gonna make an example of her before da feds got too much intel, but she turned da tables on them. By some wild, crazy fluke, she somehow shot all four of da guys who were going to debone her. She musta went nuts, killed four hardasses dead, all by herself. That got people on all sides nervous, an' everyone wanted it kept quiet fast. It was weird cuz those were four hard, gun guys too," Frank said.

"Do you guys actually know how sick and fucked up you all are? You're a vomit stain on humanity! Are you even capable of introspection?" Wade asked.

"You ain't exactly Santa Claus yourself."

"So what's the game here with Feland, the little black rings, this prison colony, and the graves? What gives? It doesn't look like prostitution exactly, and you aren't getting many new cult members. The ones you keep don't work or provide much. Is it just to sell live torture theatre tickets? You're performing this macabre shit to the same audience until those kids die? Do you know what that makes you?" Wade asked in disbelief.

"I know, I know."

"I don't think you do. If I let you live, I've got friends who'd probably want me dead just for sparing you because you're a sick, demented animal. Those kids are entirely innocent! Every moral compass in the world screams that I should kill you. I'm not like you though; you are an inhuman abomination! Do you get that?" Wade chastised.

"Yeah, yeah, and I never joined the Glee Club either, so what?" Frank asked.

"Who else is working with you besides Feland?" Wade asked.

"Nah, that's it."

"Try again, Frank, and don't piss me off. Someone was with you in the tunnel. Your steps were the heavy ones, and someone with very light steps slipped by me to make me turn around. So either you tell me right now the names of everyone involved, or you'll be screaming 'til your voice gives out!"

Just then, a steady voice came over the public address system. There were two large speakers mounted high above the torture chair for reinforcement.

"Alright, that will do, Frank. No more," the voice said.

A precision shot from a gun with a silencer made a small, sharp piercing sound within a dull "whumph!" before Frank's head tilted back and then fell forward, gushing blood straight down his face.

"A Mexican standoff, then, is it?" the voice asked.

Wade hid behind the chair and worked his way into the little cleanup room beside it.

"I know that's you, Feland! I recognize your voice!"

"Alright then, as I said, a Mexican standoff, Mr. Wade Axtol! Well, I'd wager you'd wished you had a cell phone with you earlier today, but we all have our proclivities, don't we? You want answers? Well, alright, whenever you don't like what you see, look up, straight up to those who can afford to implement such things, to those you trust, to the established and wealthy. The ones you see on television, the ones who need your vote and forget you the moment they have it. Look for those who tell you how to behave and what you can say and what you can't. Look for power but never try to rattle it without proper insurance, or you may find it unbearably expensive, I wonder if you didn't leave any DNA from beneath your fingernail under Frank's eyelid," Feland said.

"A drop in the bucket compared to what levels of missing DNA that'd be found on this property!"

"You won't call the cops, not with your methods, or you would have done so already,"

You think you can rattle me into coming out in the open while you take pot shots at me?" Wade shouted.

"Not at all. You are an annoying case of infection that won't go away. Even your cheap joke on the golf club you sent that read 'Noel Feland,' or No L. Feland, implying my demise. It was tacky and sophomoric. You are not from our sector, not from the underworld, neither an ex-con nor a fed, and not even a mercenary. You are an annoying, living blister that bubbled up after a jog, an insect on the food at the picnic. One that continuously flutters just out of range from the flyswatter. You had us all fooled into suspecting you might be a foreign asset of some kind, and you are nothing but an uncultivated commoner: a dyspeptic little orphan who bites people when he fights. Alright, you uncouth little irritant, you've had your fun. Now it's time to run along. You are out of your depth," Feland said.

"What about you, Feland? What's your story? A depravity merchant with little black rings for your cronies who were too misanthropic for school? Then the same insignia on your ring is carved into Craven's body. Aren't you just some pathetic version of a Reaver wannabe? You're too smart to believe all the hocus pocus around this stuff, so what's your draw?" Wade asked.

"That's a story for another day, I'm afraid. I don't care about you. You are uneducated, spectacularly unimpressive, and beyond uninteresting. Still, you have the ulcer-like tendency to inconvenience your betters, so I'm prepared to offer you your life if you can realize it's time to leave well enough alone. You've won all your little scraps; you dodged law enforcement, a trained military squad, and now Frank. I can see you may well be an inexquisite problem that I don't need, with your little gang of... what? Shoplifters, amateur card hustlers, feral delinquents, or deranged audiophiles with insistent musical tastes? I don't care. I don't want them ignorantly coming to avenge you or sneaking out of some grimy little sewer hole to surprise me. You walk today, and I leave you alone for good. Same with your little gang of miscreants.

You leave this place to me and my business alone forever. Do we have a deal?" Feland asked.

"You forgot unvaccinated. I'd need to know that your twisted, little torture carnivals are gone forever."

"Stay out of it, and there's twenty thousand in it for you. Last chance!" Feland said in more of a squawk than a shout.

"You didn't really think I was dumb enough to come here alone, did you?" Wade asked, bluffing.

"Later!" Feland said, bolting from the upper landing, slamming a door behind him as Wade listened to the pattern and timing between the man's steps to gauge his pace and project distance, but soon they were too faint. Being unarmed and counting himself lucky, he adjusted his vision goggles and then carefully left for home in the opposite direction.

CHAPTER 16

BROKEN PATHS AND A FIXED FUTURE

Mrs. Macharest called, looking to confirm some rescheduled dinner plans, sounding unusually chipper.

"Oh, Wade, you simply wouldn't believe the progress Vicki has made. I'm astonished she's reading scores of books at a time now, and she has such a positive attitude after all she's been through, but she needs some friends. I'm just an old goat to someone her age; that's why it'll be so good for her to see you and Deneige and talk about different things other than who was president the last time I did something adventurous," Mrs. Macharest said.

"Okay, tell her we want to see her; we just have a few details to work out first, okay?"

"Okay, I'm just telling you that she talks about you two all the time. Well, more of you, really, but she'd love to see you guys," she said.

"Oh, someone's here; I'll call you back," Wade said.

Deneige entered, wearing a black blazer with a purple blouse and her hair put up in curls, exposing her neck.

"Hey, good lookin'! My friend Sasha from Manhattan has opened a restaurant, and we're invited. The mayor is coming, and there's going to be some celebrities from Hollywood. Everything is on the house for us, and she just wants a few people there that she can count on. Sound fun?" Deneige asked.

"Sure, I wish I'd known because we've put off Mrs. Macharest a few times now, and Vikki needs a few ears from her own generation to talk to, and I don't like ditching people, so I'm afraid I committed and said we'd go," Wade said.

"Well, sure, but can't we go another night? This is a pretty big deal for my friend, and they're footing the bill for us; it would look beyond rude if we said no, right?" Deneige asked.

"You sure look nice, but it's almost like you made your decision to go before we even talked it over," Wade said with a mild grin.

"So we can go and rub elbows with people who have a future in this city and learn and grow, or we can watch children's programs and babysit someone who is supposed to be an adult. Now we're struggling with it. What to do?" Deneige said.

"That young woman was abused for years, and we can't even make time for one single visit to ask how she is keeping?" Wade asked.

"I wouldn't use the word 'keeping,' Wade; you might trigger your friend," Deneige said.

"Look, I understand. You have a pal that needs you, and you want to keep your word, as do I, and I am not trashing your friend by calling her shallow, pretentious, or anything like that," Wade said.

"Shallow and pretentious from someone who doesn't even have a car? Maybe you should go hang out with Grams and her new client, patient, or whatever she is," Deneige said.

"Okay, how about you go to your venue, and I'll go to mine?" Wade said.

"You're really going to leave me unattended at an event full of wealthy men and go-getters?"

"Yup, I'm going to go hang out with the runt of the litter because, you know what? No one would want to walk a single step in her shoes, and I'm not going to judge her."

"You are serious! Are you going to leave me at the altar too?" Deneige asked.

"Mrs. M. did a lot for me, and that girl who had absolutely nothing to her name gave me the only thing she had as a thank you. You may consider her less than impressive, and maybe most people wouldn't argue with you. I don't see it that way, and I'm going to make an appearance in her life. I love New Yorkers, I really do; I love the accent, the culture, all of it, but the last one I met was a perverse monster in human form. If I were more cynical, I'd ask your friend if she knew him. Of course, that's a long way from here and wouldn't likely go over, so I can live with myself if I miss one event," Wade said.

"Well, aren't you just the most suspicious person to ever live? What's next? Are you going to accuse my grieving parents of something too? Ask them if they've been to New York lately in case they're sickos. Do you want to know how disturbed they are, Wade? They play lottery tickets! That's the worst thing they do. Why don't you pound on their door and make sure the numbers aren't rigged? Right away, go! What are you waiting for?" Deneige asked.

"Look, your parents are fine, and you are fine, but you are a social climber, and I'm just a regular Joe at best. That lifestyle holds no value for me. Why fight to get to the top of the machine if you don't admire the machine? I want to get a small piece of land one day and maybe a cabin and do artwork or something like that, and I need somebody who would be okay with that life. I'm not into the jet set or one to follow gossip columns, and I couldn't fake it for someone if they were. Can you understand?" Wade asked.

"Oh, I understand, alright. You are dumping me. You are leaving me-ee! No one has ever left me before unless I decided it. This is new for me. You don't even have a car, and you are choosing the highway of endless uncertainty and being alone over me. I'm speechless. Really!" Deneige said.

"I only—"

"There is no way you are seriously leaving me over this! Do you realize what you're giving up? You're throwing us away," Deneige said.

"Sometimes….Summer is a moonlit kiss that lasts until dawn. Autumn is the embrace that follows, and then it's gone," Wade responded evenly.

"What a lovely and eloquent thought from yet another side of you that I never got to see. In the early stages of dating, it's all wining and dining, chocolates, flowers, and maybe poetry, and on the way out, you get a two-line tease of a rhyme scheme that doesn't even measure up to a sonnet. Am I to accept your two-second, table-napkin loquacity as a reflection on the magnitude of what two people can feel in such a moment? Of course, that's wrong now; I should have said one person!"

Riley came in and started barking loudly. Wade took him into the next room and closed the door.

"I'm sorry; he's not used to people fighting. As unrefined as our lot is, we get along pretty well, or we did, I should say. Suzette wants me to give her away at the wedding. Would you still want to attend that?" Wade asked.

"The reason you climb to the top of the machine is that if you don't have enough money to protect you, the machine just might steamroll right over you. We all face choices in terms of where we cross the finish line in life. There is the elite, the wealthy, the upper middle class, middle, middle lower, and lower class; if determining one's path to ascent is of no consequence to you, then the gutter beckons," she said.

Deneige walked over to the door and wound up her arm to slam it shut but stopped and collected herself. She put her hand over her eyes so that Wade couldn't see and closed the door gently.

Wade felt in need of a change of circumstances. Feland was still at large; the manor might be activated again. It still remained largely intact despite the temporary police presence, which had since dissipated. Wade knew it meant either a higher-level investigation was going on, waiting for Feland to screw up before they brought him down, or he had powerful authorities protecting him. Deneige was now gone; his team, which had served above and beyond every time, was gone; and once again, he saw the world as a wide-open backyard. He took Riley with him and hitchhiked to Mrs. Macharest's place, eager to find some peace.

They ate outside on a picnic bench, enjoying steak and potatoes with gravy. The portions were generous, and there was a sign saying "Welcome Back Wade" on the porch extension. Vikki glanced at the pendant she gave him but didn't mention it.

"Oh, I want to thank you, Vikki, for giving me this, and I'm sure you know I am not a spiritual person, but I'm not a nihilist either. I believe in people and family and that there are goodhearted ones among us every day if we are willing to look. I was in a tough moment introspectively, let's say, and I saw your pendant in a moment of doubt, and I remembered how you persevered after all you went through, and it gave me the boost in courage to get me through a personal trial, and that was significant, believe me," Wade said.

Vikki laughed uproariously as she had been a bit giggly throughout the dinner, but that nearly made her cough up her food.

"Forgive me, but you had an epiphany. Metaphorically speaking, you saw a symbol that represented the suffering of another, and that boosted your faith to help you over an emotional hurdle. This is what Christians call a religious experience; they hold the cross to give them the inspired strength of Christ to bolster their courage and faith. That's exactly what you've described. It really was like an atheist's cross then," she said, fighting back more laughter.

"Well, I don't know what kind of drugs Mrs. Macharest has been feeding you, but what happened to the whole 'I don't know much,' friendly, nonjudgmental kid I met? Now you've got this vocabulary, all these insights, and powers of observation that leave me a little gun-shy. This is terrible. Switch her back, Mrs. M., switch her back," Wade said, laughing.

"Now you know why I wanted someone else to be on the receiving end of her arguments. She corners me with logic problems every day, and she's not a kid anymore; did you know that she's nineteen now?" Mrs. Macharest asked.

"No, but she sounds like she has been reading for seventy years."

"Mrs. Macharest told me how many books you read when you stayed here, and I used you as my blueprint and added one book per week so that I could surpass you, with respect, of course," Vikki said.

"Books are knowledge; Milton's essay "Areopagitica" is one of the most important things I've ever read," Wade said.

"Often paired with "On Liberty" by John Stuart Mill as the cornerstones of free-thinking societies and individuals alike," Vikki said.

"I'm impressed," Wade said.

"What aspect did you find most compelling about his work? Was it the way he used reason to quell the book burners, the way he diverted religious dogma, or the fact that centuries after his death, his words were put into English law? They might well be the only reason you and I are allowed to read anything that doesn't fall under the umbrella of religious authoritarianism."

"Who are you? What happened? Last time I saw you, you said the word 'tattoo,' and now you are a shameless egghead. I think it's a beautiful thing. I'm proud of you and impressed out of my socks, but a little baffled," Wade confessed.

"Mrs. Mach, as I call her, noticed that I was drinking up the books too fast and got a tutor from the library to come visit on Wednesdays for an hour; then it became two, and then it was whole afternoons until one day she said she couldn't help me anymore because I'd shot past her, so that was sad but a little uplifting at the same time. I'm a shameless bookworm, actually," Vikki said.

"And how are you feeling in your new life these days?"

"I feel like the world is full of wonder and strange answers. Nature is so beautiful to carefully study, but some of the toxins come from the loveliest plants and animals, and those, in turn, provide some of the best medicines. Some days I just want to explore every cave, mountain peak, or meadow and have nature teach me all her secrets. I don't think it could be done in a lifetime," she said.

"Intellectual points with just a light dash of emotional flavor and never overdoing it. Wow! What a living gem you've helped polish, Mrs. Mach," he said.

"She looks nicer too, with her hair cut all nice 'n' wavy like that and in a proper dress. Some young guy is going to come along and scoop her up before she even knows it, don't you think?" Mrs. Macharest asked.

Wade took notice of her soft, expressive blue eyes, engulfed by waves of chestnut-feathered hair, and lively smile. He wondered again how blind he'd been before never to have noticed.

"Undoubtedly," Wade said.

"What men? Mrs. Macharest moved into the 'horses and squirrels only' section of the world, and it all but says so on the map, the only scooping happening involve horses," Vikki scoffed.

Wade took a moment to ponder how happy and harmless Vikki was. She'd been through the worst a human could endure, and she bore no bitterness or resentment toward the world around her. He wondered if he could measure up in terms of becoming a better person. Wade was the last to surrender his grueling career of exposing evil, which was so fraught with risks that it barely made sense. Additionally, he craved lightheartedness, to be around someone who was unabashedly kind and gentle in spirit—someone who, by their very nature, could cleanse him of the evil residue that crept into his soul just from constant exposure. If such a person existed, she was sitting directly across from him.

"Well, I've got a big double wedding to go to, and it's coming up soon, if you can excuse the offensively short notice," Wade said.

"Really? You want me to go with you? I've never been to a wedding before! Something blue, right? Oh my, I have to go read up on wedding protocol! Isn't there dancing? I've never danced! Oh my, oh my. I'll be right back!" Vikki said, laughing.

She ran from the table, and Mrs. Macharest walked by Wade with the smuggest grin he'd ever seen on her.

"You didn't have to throw us together into a fish barrel like that, you know," Wade said.

"Who, me? I stayed in the kitchen the whole time. I can't even imagine what you're talking about," she said.

If summer was a moonlit kiss that lasted 'til dawn, then the moon was a silent witness to countless vows exchanged between young lovers. On this night, the moon was full of bared souls, confessed desires, and open hearts with no fear of autumn or even winter. At daybreak, the sunlight proudly boasted of its healing powers and promises of unending tomorrows.

For all the starlit sky promises and morning glow flowers that bloomed and reflected the lovers' mood with colors of rose-petal red and candy-corn yellow draped in aromatic scents, elsewhere the sky remained darker than a dreamless sleep. Balcom Manor still stood as a protected monument, and as such, it couldn't be destroyed. Ownership faced some fines and health code violations, but ultimately it stood as it had for over two hundred years. Within its walls, Feland was having a terrific argument on the phone.

"You've cost us, Feland! Too much. Too many mistakes, too much word getting out, too much money lost, and too many excuses."

"All of these things can be fixed; the property is still here, and with a few staff replacements, I can remedy all of this in short time," Feland said.

The back door to his office opened, and he saw a handheld crossbow that launched a dart into his collarbone instantly. He immediately ripped the dart from where it had lodged and tossed it aside.

"What's in the dart?" he shouted into the phone as the door closed behind him.

"It's Carfentanil," the voice answered.

"Carfentanil! That's for tranquilizing elephants! It'll kill me!" Feland shouted in exasperation.

"True, and while it's a hundred times stronger than fentanyl, that's exactly what the cops will think it is once we get a few laxatives in you. They never check the debris that runs out of you. That'll be just enough time to carve our little signature monogram into your skin, and in a few minutes after that, it won't matter."

Feland got up, ran to look out the window, took his handkerchief, and wiped his brow. He walked past his desk and, in an attempt to stabilize himself with his hand, fell. He was still awake but slowing and groggy as his door opened again, and he heard the same voice from the phone speaking out loud.

"I'll take that!"

Defiantly, he motioned to clutch at his phone and then to push back against the hands undressing him, but his limbs wouldn't respond to his will. Like a bystander at their own funeral, all he could do was watch his demise be played out, only with methodical precision.

A series of intricate cuts were carved into his body, and he was unable to even protest by screaming as no voice could be mustered from his throat. He tried in vain to fight the overwhelming desire for sleep. He felt the pain but couldn't speak, move, or resist; he was a mere vessel to entertain the variety of sadism he'd so often engineered. It wasn't quite regret he felt but more betrayal and self-loathing, and his only regret was having overlooked such a capable and lethal adversary. His hubris allowed for one that he'd considered too harmless to reach him. After pouring some salt into his mouth, followed by a handful of laxatives, and allowing him his last sips of water, the killer savoringly watched the expression fade from his eyes. Feland lay locked in pain, staring, very much alive yet unable to even blink. He still felt superior to his adversary until he saw the aroused sense of delight in the killer's eyes as she left him with one final thought.

"The most vile and evil hellspawn ever born out of Balcom Manor to walk this earth was never my sister, you ignorant fool. It was me!" she said.

CHAPTER 17

TWO VISIONS OF THE AFTERLIFE

The house had begun as a simple four-wall-and-ceiling project on a large stretch of rented Crown Land. Within two years, Wade had built himself an impressive and expansive home. He didn't do it alone, of course; he had help from his wife, Vikki, and other visiting friends from time to time. Jake and Ray came by often at first, but as Jake's racing career gained steam, Ray joined him as a member of his pit crew. They had lives on their own, and both had several children to keep them busy. Their wives, Suzette and Angel, maintained a friendship with Vikki, only interrupted by distance and duties. Cody came by several times and helped with roofing. He usually refused to take any money, and when Wade grew insistent, Cody would raise his hand and wave his index finger at him as a private joke to suggest he'd rather have his fingers broken than accept a fee. He occasionally found little stacks of sealed money on the grounds that he accepted as fair gain. Riley would collect broken branches, expecting they might build the house with them. They served as kindling instead. Stan made an out-of-the-blue appearance, rolling up on his loud monster hog, all road-weary and worn but somehow looking even tougher than before.

They laughed away an afternoon, and then Stan made good on his promise and disappeared into the other side of the horizon. Suzette and Angel opened a small restaurant together, and Jake's pit crew ate there often. Cody eventually left to stay with Mrs. Macharest, and while he showed no interest in her book attic, he enjoyed the physical work and bonding with the horses, filling Vikki's absence happily.

The expecting couple were confident in their decision to live remotely out in nature, which was ideal for Wade to sculpt and paint, and it was great when the guests kept coming. Once the house was complete, however, and people's lives became more full, the question of going too far from society occasionally gave them pause.

Vikki was now pregnant with twins, and one day as they sat on the lawn swing, listening to the birds and frogs and the running of the nearby stream, she had questions.

"I believe in respecting people's privacy and giving them their space, but we're about to have two children now, and I'd like to ask about some things I've never understood. I hoped we might discuss them today and perhaps never bring them up again. Would you be okay with that?" she asked.

"Of course, I've got no secrets from you; go ahead," Wade said.

"Well, I've been having these dreams at night about your ex, Deneige, and she was so beautiful and majestic and all these things. Why did you two part?"

"Relationships are built on trust; I'd say we had some trust issues and wanted different things out of life. What kind of dreams?" he asked.

"Disturbing ones. The kind where Denieige never dies and comes after me and threatens me. She says I stole her internal mate and that no one steals from her without paying the price. Then she claims that our babies are rightfully hers, and she's going to take them back from me, no matter what. She kills them horribly and changes their names when they become demons. Then I wake up; it's the same recurring dream each time," Vikki said.

"That's a harrowing dream to have even once, let alone recurring."

"There's more. She claimed to own you, and you can never be free from her," she added.

"Well, demons aren't real, and you can't have stolen anything that came to you by their own free will. I chose you, not her, and that's final. What did you tell her?"

"I told her I wasn't going to fight with her and that I was on a higher spiritual plane. She could try all she liked, but she couldn't compete with decency," Vikki said.

"When did these dreams start?"

"Everyone had them at the manor, they'd play this droning sound and a voice would come over the speakers telling us not to fear the chair,"

"Overt repetition and probably some subliminal messages as well. That's a fine bit of lucid dreaming when you answered her. When pregnancy occurs, the hormones act up quite a bit, but those are very odd and specific dreams to have. They may have purposefully suggested warped and twisted ideas to plant them in your subconscious. It's time we read up on that," he said.

"I've been reading up on trauma recovery, but c'mon, Wade, I really want to know what happened between you two."

"There were a number of things, some small and some more troubling. Firstly, she was the only person Riley, my silent dog, consistently barked or growled at. We wound up on a property owned by an old woman acting like a stranger, but I could tell they knew each other beforehand. When I asked her what she cared about most, she told me about an imaginary being, not her sister or any living person. She was gleefully careless with private matters, and her old crony Margie, was siphoning intel for Feland. At one point, he had a gun on me but wanted to let me go. He knew all sorts of things about me that no one would ever tell him. It wasn't like our group to spill information, so who was the newest member in the fold? Deneige, and her alone. She had access to everything, and everyone trusted her. It wouldn't be too far a stretch for her to prep him or his henchmen when our backs were turned. That's how the fixer found us all. She said her parents 'served their roles' like they were her subjects or employees. She probably wanted to kill us all by her own hands," he said.

"That's a pretty harsh accusation, but she certainly wasn't the person you all thought she was. Did you love her?" Vikki asked.

"No, she reminded me of someone else. She represented a shadow image lost in time, one that could never line up with reality. We are out of that line of work now and need to focus on you being healthy and happy and building our family together. With your sunshine smile and my Book of the Month Club membership, we're going to have a family and raise them properly. The nature of the work leads to a certain amount of paranoia; if you ignore it completely, you end up in a pine box. If you listen to it and make decisions based on it, you end up delusional and camped out in a rubber room. When Feland died, that was the last anyone heard about their cults. I knew of no boss he answered to and no distant figure in charge of him, so then who killed Feland, ritual style? The internet said there were people the police wanted to question, and she was never seen again. If I were to listen to my paranoid side, I could entertain a few theories."

"Like?" Vikki saked.

"Deneige claimed to be an atheist but referred to supernatural events as taking place up there or down here in the present tense. That doesn't wash. Suzette gets humiliated by some girls led by one named Sasha, also the name of her friend who, after some squabbles with the police, suddenly had enough money to open a restaurant. When I first asked her if the cult had contacted her, she never answered perhaps because she was running it. Deneige also said the authorities had been leaning hard on her parents and worried that people might accuse them of wrongdoing. What if they changed their name from Balcom to St. James over prior problems at the manor? If Balcom, the St. James's fixer, was a relative who became expendable after he met Feland, the wealthy demonologist, who provides some big-name clients until Balcom starts attracting too much attention flashing his cash around. What if her parents were the ones providing pets and buying the toys to lure the kids into the pit chair? They got off on watching the torment as their captives lamented over saving their pets, collecting new toys, or ending up in that chair. The sickos could justify any torture as punishment to ease their guilty consciences. Melanie and Deneige's parents may have simply loved dark psychological experiments. Treat one daughter brutally and lavish the other with love and favor. After Melanie's constant punishment, she ran for it, so they decided to teach Deneige the art of manipulation and how to get whatever she wants so she'd never run or want to expose them. When Balcom gets left in the lurch, no one went to help because he'd become a risky embarrassment. When we left him on that roof for the cops, we did them a favor, but they had to take it further. Then Feland suddenly knows everything about us, courtesy of Deneige, and even a random carjacker needs data on me like where I went to school. When the feds come looking for Feland and he can't wiggle away unless he gives them something, so he tosses them her parents in exchange for immunity, and now there is only one motivated person left to kill him: Deneige! So you couldn't have been more apropos when you said she could never compete with decency. She could never even enter that arena against you; she is devoid of all the abundant lovable qualities you exude every day. Of course, without any of her crew left to buffer her crimes and the police involved, these notions are all just paranoid and unprovable thought exercises I'd normally keep to myself. I'm cleansing my soul of all that noise, all the fighting, the strategies, and the stresses. I'm all done with rabbit-hole thinking forever now. If not, I'd say she was still in that black-walled, boarded-up manor, starting the whole process all over again from scratch. In reality, however, the manor has been locked down by the law. I wouldn't even be shocked if Jake and Angel burn it to the ground one day. Deneige probably met some guy with a fat wallet in a hot sports car seeking a pretty girl to help him spend his money. He'll be thrilled until he finds out she is a fugitive on the lam looking to cross any state line in record time."

He took Vikki into his arms and squeezed her, smiling warmly.

"I saw her picture on the news; they're really looking hard for her. She still knows a lot about us. Do you think she'll ever come back to get even?" Vikki asked.

"No, I'd say we can remove all of her power by simply forgetting she ever existed," Wade said.

The End